The Ballad
of
Walker Owens

The Ballad

of

Walker Owens

A Novel

Greg M. Dodd

HARVEST
CHRONICLES

ACKNOWLEDGMENTS

This is my father's story. Although, it may be more fitting to say it's a story about my father's story and the events related to it. As to its veracity, that's for you, the reader, to decide. But as my father likes to say, whether you believe it or not doesn't change the truth.

— Daniel Johnson

"Time stole you away from me
But someday I know
My song will bring you back to me."

– Walker Owens, *Escape*

PROLOGUE

The story of Walker Owens begins and ends with my father, Phillip Johnson. For as long as I've known him, my father's life has been a model of quiet predictability. That's not a criticism, just an observation. He's never been one to seek out excitement or attention, always preferring the background over the limelight. For example, in his early thirties, he purchased an established, locally owned coffee shop in Columbia, South Carolina which he renamed the Lost Bean. But despite spending countless hours in his café over the years, even some of his regular customers are often surprised to learn that he's the owner. He prefers to remain unknown, to blend in. And unlike many small business owners who lose themselves to their work, my father has always found a balance between business and family to the satisfaction of both.

That balance gave my father time for fun, silly things with me as I grew up. Like sneaking both of us out of the house after my mom was asleep to play paintball in the darkness of our backyard. Or dressing us up for Halloween one year like Doc Brown and Marty McFly from *Back to the Future* (I was Marty). Still, my dad has been a bit of an enigma to me in other ways. Apart from his business, there are two very unrelated things he obsesses over. One is time travel theory. And the other is my mother.

In his study, a room in their house I have rarely ventured into, are books written by quantum physicists with titles like *Time Travel in the Einstein Universe*, *A Brief History of Time*, and *The Science of Time Travel*. I always thought it was a strange interest for a coffee shop owner. But I just assumed he pursued the study of quantum mechanics as some sort of intellectual palate cleanser from the daily minutia of his business.

And it wasn't just books. We watched every movie you can think of that dealt with the idea of time travel. *The Time Machine*, *Somewhere in Time*, *The Terminator*, *Planet of the Apes*, and of course *Back to the Future* just to name a few. We rented *Time Bandits* back when renting movies from a store was still a thing, but he thought it was so bad he turned it off after the first twenty minutes. I've still never seen the whole movie. And he only liked the first *Back to the Future*. He dismissed the sequels as thoughtless Hollywood drivel. But he didn't just watch these films. He seemed to study them. If you watched with him, you weren't allowed to talk until the credits rolled. And of course, after each viewing – and we watched each of them several times – he'd always put on his amateur quantum physicist hat and tell me about each movie's time travel continuity errors. And he was serious. And that made it even funnier to me. Not that I laughed, mind you. I could tell the accuracy of the concept was important to him for some reason.

And then there's my dad's affection for my mom. They've been married for thirty-six years, but whenever they're together you can see a subtle giddiness in my dad that tells you he's happy and grateful to have found her. Their marriage is like a perpetual first date. It's fun to see.

Another relevant note about my father involves his occasional hobby of writing. Always a storyteller, my father self-published his first novel ten years ago. But he put no effort into marketing and sold only a few hundred copies. His primary satisfaction came from seeing his creative efforts in physical form resting on the coffee table in his den. After two more self-published, largely unread novels, he decided it was finally time to resurrect a story idea he'd been rolling around since before I was born: time travelers from the future involved in the JFK assassination. He called it *The Kennedy Axium*. Confident he had a unique, marketable story, he educated himself on the inner workings of the traditional publishing industry. He gained agent representation and saw his manuscript submitted to several publishing houses. Sadly, the only publisher still giving it serious consideration has concerns over thematic similarities with Stephen King's novel *11/22/63*. His agent has told him not to get his hopes up.

Over the last year, my father has been slowly removing himself from the daily operations of the Lost Bean. His public reason for doing so was simply to spend more time with his wife, but I've learned that other factors may have influenced his decision. In the year approaching his sixty-first birthday, I began getting reports from my mother over small changes in his behavior and memory. Little things that made her worry. Like finding his car keys in the refrigerator, forgetting people's names, or watching him struggle to write a check for the water bill. I try to reassure her, but I've also noticed small changes.

As far as I can tell, my dad's long-term memory seems unaffected. But his short-term memory has become a little fickle. So, while he can tell you in great detail – assuming his memory is accurate – about his rafting trip in Colorado twenty years ago, he'll often repeat questions or comments within the same conversation. My mom is quick to call him on it, thinking she can somehow fix his memory. But I've learned to just roll with it, even if it means acting as if I hadn't already answered the same question multiple times. It doesn't happen every time we talk, but it has become more frequent.

Earlier this year, my mother asked me to take him to their family doctor for a physical. He refused to go, saying he wasn't going to pay someone to tell him he's getting old. So, my mom and I are left to play the memory game with Dad.

As for me, I teach history at a private high school, and my summers are usually carefree. But shortly after classes ended this year, my father called and asked me to come over for a "talk." He wouldn't explain over the phone but said it was important that I come while my mother wasn't home. So, on a Wednesday night in early June, I made my way over to my parents' house for our talk. And that's where the story of Walker Owens begins.

CONTENTS

ONE

The Talk

The last time my father said we needed to have a "talk," it was *The Talk* when I was twelve. The one about the birds and the bees. I don't remember who was more uncomfortable, him or me. But as we sat on our porch steps overlooking the backyard, we struggled through it together, both of us happy to have checked that coming-of-age box after the longest five minutes of my life. But almost twenty years later, a second "talk" awaited.

I steered my car gently through the curves of my parents' quiet suburban neighborhood with my brown and white Cocker Spaniel, Bono, hanging his head out my window. I was fairly confident the topic of discussion that evening would have nothing to do with birds or bees, which sent my mind scrolling through the usual list of worst-case scenarios. I'm pretty sure I inherited that trait from my mother.

Leaving my car in the driveway, I led Bono through the garage and into the house to find my father in the kitchen searching through the pantry trashcan. Their Golden Retriever, Pumpkin, ran into the kitchen to greet us before escaping down the hall with Bono in hot pursuit. "Hey, Dad," I said.

Seeming a bit frustrated, my dad slid the trashcan back under the shelf and welcomed me in. "Hey, Son. Thanks for coming over."

I tossed my keys on the kitchen counter as I watched him stare at the trashcan. "Lose something in the trash?" I asked.

"Oh, no. I was just…" He snapped himself out of his trashcan dilemma and turned to me. "How are you?"

"I'm good. Just glad summer's finally here. Where's Mom tonight?"

"This is her women's group night at church. She'll be gone for a couple of hours. I wanted us to have the house to ourselves. You want something to drink?"

"No, I'm fine," I said, anxious to learn the reason for my visit. "So, what's going on, Dad?" I asked, following him into the den. "Is everything OK?"

"Have a seat, Son. Can I get you something to drink?"

To avoid hearing the question a third time, I said, "Iced tea would be great."

"Sure, let me get that for you," he said as Pumpkin and Bono came bounding into the room.

I sat on the couch petting the dogs while I studied our family pictures scattered around the den shelves. My dad returned with my iced tea and took a seat in his favorite chair.

"So, what's up, Dad?" I asked, trying to set a light tone for the discussion.

"Well," he said, sounding a bit hesitant, "I have something important to talk with you about."

"Uh-oh, this sounds serious."

"It is in a way. It's of a very personal nature, Daniel, and I'm hoping you'll be open to what I have to say."

"You're kind of scaring me, Dad. Are you and Mom OK? You're not getting a divorce, are you?"

He laughed and said, "No, we're not getting a divorce. You have nothing to worry about there."

"Is it cancer? You don't have cancer, do you?"

"For heaven's sake, Son. You jumped straight to the two worst things I could possibly think of."

"Then it is cancer?"

"No, it's not cancer. I don't have cancer. Geez. You're just like your mother sometimes."

I had to concede his point there. "OK, so what is it, then?"

"Well, I have a story of sorts, and I need your help writing about it."

"That's it?" I asked, relieved but slightly annoyed by its insignificance compared to divorce or cancer. "You need my help writing? Dad, you're the author. Why do you need my help?"

"Son, I don't like to admit this, particularly around your mother, but I'm not quite as sharp as I used to be. I'm sure you've probably noticed."

I sipped my tea and lied, "No, not at all."

"Oh, come on. I know your mother calls you anytime I can't remember something or can't find my wallet. It's embarrassing."

"Well, I did hear about the car keys in the refrigerator."

"I honestly don't know how that happened."

"Mom's just worried, Dad."

"I know. But the reason I called you over here is important to me, and I want to keep it between us for now, OK? Your mom doesn't need to know about this."

"OK. It's our secret. So, what's the big mystery?"

He shifted slightly in his chair before beginning. "Well, you know how I've always been interested in time travel."

"Of course."

"I've read books about it; we've watched movies."

"I know, those were fun."

"They were. But I want you to know the reason for all that."

"OK. I'm listening."

After a pause, he said, "I did it myself."

"You did what yourself?"

"I traveled in time."

I chuckled and asked, "Cool, where'd you go? Or is it when?"

"You don't believe me, do you?"

"Am I supposed to?" The lack of expression on his face caused me concern. "Wait, you're not serious."

"I am serious."

"You think you traveled in time."

"I did travel in time. Twice."

"Twice. OK. Sure. Look, Dad, what's this all about?"

"Son, I know how this sounds."

"I don't think you do," I said, my anxiety rising quickly.

He looked down for a moment before saying, "Daniel, there's a lot I want to explain to you."

"You're really serious," I said, still hoping it was all a joke.

"I'm really serious."

"Dad, I've been sticking up for you with Mom, defending your decision not to see a doctor and telling her not to worry about your memory. But this? How can I tell her not to worry about this?"

"Because you're not going to tell her about this."

"Are you sure you didn't just imagine it or have a dream about it or something? Did you watch *Back to the Future* recently?"

"Son, this isn't some dream. I'm telling you the truth. This happened a long time ago. And I've never told anyone. I've kept it a secret, even from your mother."

I stayed quiet, looking away as I shook my head.

"Why do you think I've read so many books on time travel?" he asked. "And where do you think I came up with the idea for my JFK story?"

"Well, I heard the publisher thinks Stephen King's novel has something to do with that."

His demeanor shifted into defense mode. "I've never even read Stephen King's book," he said. "And I came up with my story twenty-five years before he did. I have my original notes and outline in my study to prove it. I could sue Stephen King if I wanted to."

"Dad, unless you can prove Stephen King has been in your study, I don't think you have much of a case. So, let's not get carried away, here."

"OK, fine. But just listen to me for a minute. I want to tell you about what happened. And I want us to capture it in writing, so it doesn't disappear when I do."

"Oh, you can disappear now, too?" I asked with sarcasm.

"That's not funny, Son."

"Well, what do you mean, then?"

"I mean when I die."

"Dad, you're only sixty-one. I think it's a little soon to be talking about that."

"Son, when you're in your sixties, you'll understand. Time is running short. Will you help me or not?"

I moved my attention to the dogs lying on the floor before me. Bono and I exchanged looks as I shook my head. "I don't know, Dad. I'm not sure I feel comfortable with all this. And keeping it from Mom. Maybe you really should see a doctor."

"This has nothing to do with seeing a doctor. And if I told your mother what I'm telling you now, she'd have me in a nursing home taking Aricept once a day."

"You're probably right about that."

We sat in silence for a few minutes. It seemed he was giving me a moment to process his…what's a word for an unintentional, but ridiculous, dementia-influenced lie? Anyway, I finally asked, "Let's say I play along with this. How do you see it working? What do you want me to do?"

"I want you to record our conversations like I'm doing now."

"You're recording this?"

"Yeah, on my phone here. Then we can get everything in writing and figure out how to tell the story."

"Um, you said conversations, plural. You mean you're not going to tell me everything now?"

"There's way too much for one discussion. I want you to hear everything. It's the story of my life, Son. We need to get it right. And we've got the whole summer to work on it."

"Dad, I…" I paused, unsure what else to say.

"Is all this too much for you? You think your father is going crazy?"

"I don't know what to think, Dad. I mean…time travel? You called me over here to tell me that? How did you expect me to react?"

"About like you are now," he said with a grin. "Look, Son, just keep an open mind. Will you do that for me? Please?"

I inhaled deeply and sighed it all out. "I just need to think about all this, Dad. Can you give me a day or so?"

"Why don't we just plan to meet here again next Wednesday, same time? We can talk again then."

"Fine." I stood up and headed toward the kitchen with Pumpkin and Bono following behind me. Grabbing my keys off the counter, I said to my dad, "So, you think you really did the whole Doc Brown, *Back to the Future*, *Time Bandits* thing, huh?"

"Don't get me started on *Time Bandits*; that's a terrible movie. And yes, I really did. But there's a lot more to the story than just that."

"That's what I'm afraid of."

"I'll see you next week, Son."

TWO

Meet Phillip Johnson

Over the week following my dad's decision to share his time travel delusion with me, I had given my response a lot of thought. Should I be the passive enabler and go along with his story? Or should I be the responsible caretaker and get him some help? But who would that help be? A psychiatrist? A geriatric doctor? A quantum physicist? And then there would be my mother's reaction. The thought of managing her concerns and the endless phone calls it would generate made my decision for me. After all, it was a harmless delusion. Time travel, no big deal. And we could always pass the story off as a work of fiction. I had reached an acceptable compromise with my conscience. So, I returned to my father's house the following Wednesday evening, prepared for my role of passive enabler. Bono opted to stay home.

My pen hovered over my legal pad on their kitchen table. "OK, so how do you want to start this?" I asked.

"Aren't you going to record us?" my father asked.

"Oh, yeah." I opened the voice memo app on my phone and tapped the round red button. "You're on. Go ahead." Despite recording, I still felt the need to take written notes as thoughts came to me.

"I think we need some background on the main character," my dad suggested.

"You mean you, right?"

"Yeah. Let's give an intro about me."

"And this is the real you, not some fictional you."

"Yes, the real me."

"Are we using real names?

"For now. We can always change them later."

"OK, what would you like to say about yourself?"

"Well, the basics, you know. Like where I was born, something about my family. What it was like growing up in our house."

"All right then, go ahead."

"Well, my dad, your grandfather, had served in the military before I was born."

"I don't think I knew that."

"Yep, he was in the Army. And he basically ran our house like a platoon leader. He was very regimented about everything."

"What about Grammy? She was always so sweet all the time."

"My mom was very sweet. And pretty quiet, too. But she just went along with everything my dad did. He served in the military, you know."

"Yeah, I know."

"He was very—"

"Regimented."

"Exactly."

"OK, so besides being in a mini boot camp," I said, "what was it like growing up for you and Uncle Jim and Aunt Stella and everybody?"

"You know, I've never said this to anyone, but being the youngest of five, I always wondered if I was a mistake."

"Why would you say that?"

"I was the youngest by three years. And sometimes I felt like an afterthought, just an extra kid tossed into the mix with my brothers and sisters. All the rules were already set by the time I came along. I just had to fall in line or drop and do pushups."

I laughed. "You're kidding, right?"

"No, I'm not."

"Wow," I said. I tried to imagine my dad as a little kid getting herded around with his four siblings like army recruits. "As an only child, it's kind of hard for me to relate to all that."

"Maybe it's why we stopped after we had you, I don't know."

"OK, well, anything else?"

"Why don't we start there and see how it goes."

"When does the whole, time travel thing come in?"

"We'll get to that, don't worry."

"OK, then. Let's see how this might sound if I type it up. Give me a few minutes."

I opened my laptop and stared at the screen for a moment, glancing occasionally at my notes. Then I began to type. After I finished, I turned my screen around so my dad could read. "How 'bout we say something like this," I said.

ঙ৯৶

Phillip Johnson was the youngest of five children born to James and Marilyn Johnson of Charlotte, North Carolina. His father, a tall, stoic man of upright posture and lean build, ran his family with military efficiency. His mother, a small, demure woman by nature, nevertheless governed their children with firm devotion to her husband's rigid standards. By the time Phillip was born into his parents' suburban household in the summer of 1963, there was little discussion of, or variance from, the routines and expectations already established and conformed to by his older brothers and sisters.

ঙ৯৶

"That's really good," he said, taking off his readers.

"I left out the part about doing push-ups."

"No, it's good."

"Is it OK style-wise?" I asked. "Will that work for you?"

"Sure, I like that just fine," he said. "See? You're already helping."

"That's one paragraph, Dad. We have a long way to go. What's next?"

"Why don't we jump into my childhood interests?"

"And what were those?"

"Well, let's see. By the time I was in eighth or ninth grade, I was really into drawing."

"You never told me that."

"It was just pencil sketches. But I got pretty good at it. I spent a lot of time in my room drawing. My brothers and sisters were into sports and clubs and social things like that, so I was kind of the oddball of the family."

"What kind of things did you draw?"

"Headshots, mostly. Girls from school, you know. Everybody back then would exchange class pictures. The little wallet-sized photos, the ones they took for the yearbook. Word got around about my drawings and guys started asking me to sketch their girlfriends. I did a few of them for $10 a piece until one kid, Jason Lee, got all bent out of shape about how big I drew his girlfriend's nose."

I couldn't help but laugh.

"Well, she had a big nose," he said in his defense. "You couldn't miss it. That's actually what kids called her, Brenda Big Nose."

"Oh my gosh. Brenda Big Nose?"

"Or just Big Nose for short."

"That poor girl."

"Anyway, Jason was pretty sore about it. He stopped speaking to me. So, I said no to everyone after that. It wasn't worth the trouble."

"You stopped drawing?"

"No, I kept drawing. But just things like famous people, our dog, album cover art, that sort of thing. And pretty girls I knew."

"So, is drawing pretty girls relevant to your time travel story?"

"I guess it depends on which girls you're talking about. You'll see."

"All right. Just making sure we're staying on topic."

"No, that's good; keep asking."

"So, you mentioned girls and music."

"Right. But music came first. Then girls."

ॐ

Phillip's youthful interests had been — in order of acquisition — art, music, and girls. By his early teens, he had developed a skill for drawing realistic pencil sketches. But unlike his siblings' socially engaging hobbies of sports, choir, or drama club, drawing required uninterrupted isolation. And spending hours alone at his bedroom desk without moving anything but the tip of a pencil was a discipline his family failed to appreciate. But Phillip's ability to draw portraits from photographs led many of his friends from school to seek his services. "Can you draw my girlfriend?" was the most common request. After obliging several times with happy results, a friend took issue with the size of his girlfriend's nose in Phillip's rendering. Phillip maintained that he only drew what he saw. "And she does have a big nose," he added. To avoid losing any more friends, Phillip decided to limit his subjects to celebrities, animals, and album covers.

❧❦

"So, what kind of music did you listen to growing up?" I asked. "I'm guessing disco. It was the 70s, right?"

My father laughed. "It wasn't what I listened to so much as what I played."

"What you played? What do you mean?"

"On guitar."

"You played guitar?"

"Sure."

"You don't even own a guitar."

"Yes, I do. There's one in my study. Why don't you go up there and get it for me? It's in the large cedar chest below the window."

I climbed the stairs to the second floor with Pumpkin right behind me. After opening the door to my dad's study, I let my eyes wander around the room which held such mystery for me growing up. The large antique leather top writing desk and high-back leather chair, the small navy couch facing a wall-sized bookshelf full of novels, vintage books, and of course his time travel physics collection. I opened the cedar chest by the window and found a nice, natural wood Fender acoustic guitar with mahogany back and sides. The strings were fairly loose, and a metal guitar pick was taped to the neck. I picked it up carefully and carried it back downstairs. Handing it to my dad I asked, "You can really play this?"

"It's been a long time," he said, "but let's see what my fingers can remember."

He took a couple of minutes to tighten and tune each string by ear, then cleared his throat and began strumming. To my amazement, it sounded pretty good. My dad could play guitar. But my reaction went beyond amazement when he started singing. He sang a country tune I'd never heard before, his voice sounding somewhere between Earl Thomas Conley and T. Graham Brown. The song itself was a catchy, heartfelt country ballad of conflicted love. I was dumbfounded. And confused.

When his song was over, I sat with my mouth hanging open. I chuckled and asked, "Dad, what the heck? Was that an old Brooks & Dunn song or something?"

"No, I wrote that. It's called *Give Me a Reason*."

"You wrote that," I said, shaking my head in disbelief. Then I asked, jokingly, "Who *are* you?"

As he leaned the neck of the guitar against the kitchen table, he said plainly, "Well, most people knew me as Walker Owens. *Give Me a Reason* was my first big hit."

At that, I stood up and took two or three long steps across the kitchen floor. My passive enabler head was about to explode. My father – my comforting, predictable, rock of stability – was freaking me out. His delusion was clearly escalating. Turning back to face him, I asked, "What are you saying here, Dad? That you were some kind of country music star before I was born?"

"Kind of. But it's more accurate to say I was a country music star *instead* of you being born."

"What is *that* supposed to mean?"

He raised his hand as if to say stop. "I'm sorry, Son, but I think we're getting a little ahead of ourselves, here. That's my fault. This business of time travel can get pretty confusing sometimes. Let's backup."

"Dad, I'm sorry, but I have to ask, is this some sort of elaborate *joke* you're playing on me? I feel like I'm on a reality TV show or something."

In a calming voice, he said, "No, Son, I promise. I wouldn't do that to you."

I paced around the kitchen for a moment before leaning, arms crossed, against the counter. "Dad, I think this is all I can absorb for one night. I'm sorry. I'm gonna go now. I'll just see you next Wednesday."

"No, I'll see you Sunday for lunch. It's your mother's birthday, remember?"

"Oh, crap," I said, dropping my head. As if I needed more stress at that moment. "I still need to get her something."

"And not a word to your mom about our story. Promise?"

I sighed, shook my head, and in my best enabler voice I said, "I promise, Dad."

THREE

Happy Birthday

Even on her birthday, my mother insisted on cooking Sunday dinner for us. When I arrived, the kitchen smelled of fried chicken and homemade biscuits. On the stovetop were green beans and a pot of Kraft macaroni and cheese, my favorite since I was a kid. She had even baked her own birthday cake. A five-layer red velvet masterpiece. While I was there for her – and the food – the burden of my father's emerging "life story" weighed heavily on my mind. And the temptation to reveal our secret, or at least make subtle hints at it, tightened my chest from the moment Bono and I walked in the door.

After hugs and hellos, we helped our plates, said the blessing, and began to enjoy our dinner. The conversation, led by my mother, naturally turned to the question of when I was going to propose to my girlfriend, Elizabeth. I deflected by telling a long story about Elizabeth's dog getting lost and the lucky way she found him with help from Bono and me. By the time I finished, the question of our potential engagement was ancient history.

After dinner, it was time to eat cake and open presents. I cleared the table, then watched my mother dig through the gift bag I had picked up at the pharmacy as a quick alternative to wrapping her present. She pulled out the small box inside and examined it for a moment.

"It's a juicer," I said.

"Yes, I see!" she said, doing her best to seem excited.

"You make juice with it."

"I know, that's wonderful. Thank you, Son."

"There's a card in there, too."

She reached back into the bag, opened the card, and read it out loud. It had a drawing of a smiling clothes washing machine saying, "I love you loads."

"That's so sweet," she said, looking at the card.

"That's a washing machine, get it? I love you loads?"

"Yes, I get it. It's very cute." She leaned over and gave me a hug around the neck and a kiss on my cheek. "Thank you, Son."

"OK, my turn," my father said. "But I need my guitar. Daniel, would you go look in the hall closet and grab it for me."

I got up from the table and headed down the hall as I heard my mom ask, "Your guitar? I didn't even know you still had it."

"It's been upstairs in my study," my dad said, "in my mom's old cedar chest."

"Do you remember how to play?" she asked. "It has to be thirty years since I've seen you with it."

"I guess we'll see," he said.

I returned with the guitar and handed it to my dad. "You've seen him play before, Mom?" I asked.

"Oh, yes, that's how we met," she said.

"I thought Dad asked you on a coffee date," I said as my dad began to quietly pick a few notes.

"We had coffee after one of his shows," she said.

"His shows? Like on a stage?"

"Your father was in a cover band when I was in college."

"Walker Owens?" I asked, hoping to tie in my father's story.

"Who?" she asked.

"Was that the band? Walker Owens?" I glanced at my father. He seemed surprisingly unconcerned with my question.

"No," she said, turning to my father. "What was your band called, Phillip? I can't remember."

"The Sole Winners."

"That's it," she said.

I repeated the name in my head and asked, "Was it a Christian band or something?"

"No," he said. "It was a play on words, s-o-l-e not s-o-u-l. Like we were the only winners. The name wasn't my idea."

I sat wondering if my dad had exaggerated his music experience for his story. But why would he lie to me about it?

"Anyway," he said, turning to my mother. "I decided to write you a little song for your birthday. I hope you like it."

As my father began to strum his first few chords, my mother held her hands to her cheeks in surprise. "Oh my gosh," she said. "I can't believe it! You're really playing again!"

And then my father sang in his country music voice.

Back in the day
Love was hard on me
I was up on stage
Wishing I was free

But when I sang for you
You seemed so kind
And when I walked away
I left it all behind
And there you were to save me

Oh, I love how you found me
How you wrapped your arms around me
You'll be my wife
For all my life
'til our time is gone

I'll love no one
But you.

"Happy birthday, sweetheart," he said, as he strummed his last chord. "I love you."

Tears flowed down my mother's face as she hugged my dad. "That's the most beautiful present ever," she said, wiping her face with a napkin. "Thank you, sweety."

While I felt a little embarrassed about the juicer, I realized it really didn't matter what I gave my mom that day. All she would remember was the song my dad sang for her on her birthday.

As I helped my mother clean up the kitchen, my dad disappeared somewhere in the house. "I hope you've had a nice birthday, Mom," I said, loading the dishwasher.

"Oh, it's been wonderful. And thank you for my juicer. And my card."

"I'm sorry about that. I just didn't know what to get you this time."

"You did fine. I'm sure I'll find use for it."

"That was really something, having Dad play guitar and sing for you."

"Oh, it was. I never thought he'd ever play again."

"Why is that?"

"Well, after we met and started seeing one another, he put his guitar away and said he was through with it. I haven't seen him play again until just now."

"You never asked him why?"

"We talked about it once when we were dating. He wanted to focus on finishing college and getting on with his life. I remember him saying he had dreams of being a country music singer, but they were just dreams. Besides, once your father makes up his mind about something, there's not much use in trying to change it."

It all began to click. "Just dreams, huh."

"That's what he said."

It was all I needed to hear. I gave her a kiss. "Thanks, Mom. Happy birthday."

FOUR

Just Dreams

During my initial story discussions with my father, I'd been torn between his insistence that I believe the ridiculous things he was saying and my desire to dismiss his memory issues as being trivial. The cognitive dissonance gave me headaches. Fortunately, the conversation with my mother on her birthday had given me better insight. It seemed my father was dealing with more serious aging issues than I had wanted to believe and, through his story, was giving voice to unlived fantasies of country music stardom. I didn't want to think of his mental ability deteriorating so quickly, but I had no other explanation. So, I resolved to stop reacting, arguing, judging, and worrying about what he was telling me. The fact that he wanted to believe it didn't matter. I would try again to simply listen, ask questions when necessary, and be the ghostwriter he needed me to be. The burden of truth was off my shoulders.

The Wednesday after my mother's birthday I arrived at their house with Bono, ready to jump back into our story. I found my father in the kitchen, as usual. He and Pumpkin stood before the dishwasher as white soapsuds flowed slowly over the open door onto the floor.

"Hey, Dad," I said, closing the garage door behind me.

"Hey there, Son," my dad said, staring at the wet mess.

Bono hurried over to investigate the white suds on the floor.

"What happened?" I asked.

"Oh, I must have put Dawn dish soap in the dishwasher instead of Cascade. Can you get me a couple of towels from the hall bathroom closet?"

As I walked down the hall, with Bono and Pumpkin leaving a trail of wet paw prints on the hardwood floor behind me, I couldn't help but think of my dad's soap confusion as yet another dementia episode. It just reinforced the need for patient, accepting support.

Returning with the towels to the kitchen, wiping up the dog tracks as I went, I got down on my knees and began soaking up the water and suds.

"Can we add this to the list of secrets to keep from your mother?" he asked.

I laughed. "Sure, Dad. It's in the vault."

"It's just that any and every mistake I make nowadays gets counted as evidence of my declining mental ability."

I stopped and looked up at him. Having just done that very thing, I felt guilty and slightly sorry for him. "Don't worry about it, Dad. I do stupid stuff all the time."

"I assume that's supposed to make me feel better?" he asked with a laugh.

I chuckled. "It was intended to, yeah."

He rinsed the soap off the dishes in the sink, and I put them back in the dishwasher. Trying to hover inconspicuously, I watched him pour the Cascade dishwasher detergent into the slot before closing the door and turning it on.

"You want something to drink?" he asked, drying his hands in the dishtowel.

I knew to say yes, this time. "Yes, sir. How about some iced tea?"

While he poured two glasses of tea, I wasted no time kicking things off. "So, Dad, I thought tonight we could start with your interest in playing guitar. You know, how that started, etc."

Handing me my tea, he said, "Son, before we get started, I need to apologize."

"For the dishwasher? No, don't worry about that, Dad."

"No, not that. It's just that I realize I've asked you to believe some pretty incredible things over the last two weeks, and that was unfair of me. I've put you in an uncomfortable position, and I had no right to do that."

"Dad, it's OK. I–"

"No, you have every reason to doubt what I'm saying and chalk it up to me getting old or trying to live out some delusion or fantasy. I totally get it."

I realized then that I had come to his house that night prepared to patronize him like some pathetic geriatric case. But my dad had always been a reasonable man, and that obviously hadn't changed. Perhaps he deserved more credit than I was giving him, time travel notwithstanding. "So, you don't want to keep going, then?" I asked him.

"Do you?" he asked.

"I'm interested in your story, Dad. I'd like to see where it goes."

"Why don't we just pretend that's all it is? Just a story. Would that take some of the pressure off?"

"Whatever works for you, Dad. I'm just here to help. And besides, how many sons get to write a novel with their dad?"

"I appreciate that, Daniel, more than you know. We can even tell your mom you're helping me write my last novel."

"I bet she'd be excited about that," I said.

"But let's still keep the story between us for now. Author privilege."

"Agreed," I said.

We settled in the den with our iced teas, and I began recording. Over the next hour, we talked about how he came to play the guitar and his interest in country music. I felt like I was getting to know my dad for the first time.

৩৩৹

When he was fifteen, Phillip found an unstrung acoustic guitar while exploring his parents' attic. His mother said the guitar had been a Christmas gift to his oldest brother, Jim, many years before. Jim never learned to play but had removed the strings for some forgotten reason. With his mother's permission, Phillip used his allowance money to have the guitar restrung and soon found a natural talent waiting to be explored.

Having no record player of his own, Phillip began spending any time left alone in the house in Jim's old bedroom, playing his brother's albums and trying to recreate the melodic sounds on the guitar. Encouraged but frustrated, Phillip sought beginner's guidance from his church's guitar-playing youth pastor. Practicing scales, learning chord progressions, and proper finger placement accelerated his ability to play what he was hearing.

Jim's decision to exclude his collection of country music records from those he loaded into his car after his honeymoon would steer Phillip's musical interests down a particular path cemented by his viewing of *Urban Cowboy* the summer before his senior year of high school. Artists such as George Jones, Merle Haggard, Alabama, George Strait, and Waylon Jennings became Phillip's targets of emulation. But his new hobby remained a private one.

∾∽

My mom came home a little earlier than expected. I turned off the voice memo recording and asked my dad how he wanted to explain my being there.

"Let me handle it," he said.

Coming in from the garage, my mom immediately called my name, having seen my car in the driveway.

"We're in here, Mom," I said.

"What a nice surprise; I didn't know you were coming out tonight."

I glanced at my father, and he took the cue.

"I've asked Daniel to work with me on what I'm calling my last novel. We've just been taking some notes."

"Wow, that's exciting!" she said, tossing her purse on a chair. "What story are you working on? The men's reunion weekend where the beach house burns down?"

"What's that?" I asked, interested.

My father gave a dismissive wave. "It's just an idea for a story." Turning back to my mom, he said, "No, it's something different. I haven't told you about this one."

"What's it about?" she asked.

"It's a secret," my father said, "until we get it fleshed out a little more."

My mother shrugged. "Well, you're terrible at keeping secrets," she said, turning back toward the kitchen. "I'm sure I'll find out soon enough."

My father cut his eyes at me and winked. If nothing else, we were in it together.

FIVE

Girls

It was Wednesday evening, and I had just finished dinner with Elizabeth at my house. We were hurrying to clean up after our grilled pimento cheese turkey burgers before my father arrived. My mother's women's group had been canceled, so I was hosting our weekly writing project. Elizabeth let Bono lick the plates clean before she washed them in the sink, which scored major points with me.

I had been dating Elizabeth for over two years. My mother had loved her from the start and was anxiously awaiting a daughter-in-law and grandchildren. I loved Elizabeth too, of course. But we both had careers, mortgages, pets, and interests apart from each other. Our relationship had a comfortable, predictable, healthy feel to it. Why complicate things with rings and all the decisions that come along with engagement? That was my thought anyway.

"So, you never told me how your mother's birthday went," Elizabeth said, drying a plate with my dish towel.

To avoid going into my dad's fake music career, I just said, "Oh, it was fine."

She stopped wiping the plate, smiled, and asked, "Did she like the juicer?"

"Well, she said she did. But I really owed her a better gift than that. I felt bad."

Shaking her head, she said, "I told you."

"I know, but I was in a hurry. Besides, I think she was more interested in pressing me on when I'm going to propose to you."

A grin grew on her face as she put the plate in the cabinet. "You know she asked me the same thing," she said.

"You've been talking to my mother?"

"Girls talk; you should know that."

"I feel outnumbered."

"You are. How's your dad, by the way?"

"I'm guessing my mom already told you about that, too."

"I want to hear what you think."

As we put away the last of our dinner mess, I took a moment to share my concerns about my dad's memory and mental aging issues. Elizabeth is a nurse, so I was curious about her opinion. But I left out the part about time travel and him being a country music star.

"He may be having TIAs," she said. "They're like mini strokes. From little blood clots."

"Are they serious?"

"They can be. Or they can just cause intermittent episodes. Like what you're seeing. He probably needs to be on antiplatelets."

"Anti-what?"

"Blood thinners."

"The problem is getting him to a doctor," I explained. "He's not into that."

"I can talk to him for you, if you like."

"No, that's for me to do. But thanks, though."

"If nothing else, he can at least take aspirin every day. That can help."

Before I could answer, my front doorbell rang. I knew it was my dad's formal way of announcing his arrival. I just yelled for him to come in without going to the door.

"I'll head out," said Elizabeth, picking up her purse from the counter. "Call me later?"

"Absolutely."

"Hello, Mr. Johnson," she said as my dad entered the kitchen.

"Phillip please, Elizabeth," he said, giving her a light hug.

"Got it," she said. "I was just heading out. Good to see you!"

I walked Elizabeth to the door, gave her a kiss, thanked her for coming over, then returned to the kitchen. My dad had already poured himself a glass of tea from the refrigerator.

"All right, are you ready to get started?" I asked, rubbing my hands together.

"That Elizabeth is a sweet girl," my dad said.

"She is," I agreed.

"I've noticed you do a good job of dodging your mother's questions on you two getting engaged."

I gave an awkward laugh and said, "I just don't have a good answer for that at the moment."

"Well, when the time comes, if I can help in any way, just let me know."

I had no idea what kind of help he could offer, but I thanked him, nonetheless.

Since my notepad, phone, and laptop were already on my kitchen table, we settled in there. "So," I began, "I think the topic of girls was next up. How did you want to go about that?"

"Well, I think we should just focus on the ones that matter to the story."

"Why, how many were there?"

"That's not the right question, Daniel."

"I'm sorry, I didn't mean it like that."

"Let's just take it one at a time."

"All right, I'll just shut up and listen. Go ahead."

"OK, well, for starters, there really wasn't a girl that had any particular influence on me until I got to college. And that's when everything changed."

"How so?"

"Well, in my family there were just certain expectations you didn't question or think about. One was going to college. And not just any college; we all went to the University of South Carolina. That's where my dad went, and that's where he met my mom. All four of my brothers and sisters went there ahead of me, so when I graduated from high school it was just my turn. I had no plans or ambitions about why I was there. But then one day I went to the mall to get a haircut."

I looked up from my notetaking and said, "I'm sorry, what?"

"I went to get a haircut at the mall."

"OK, you lost me."

"I'm about to tell you about a girl I met at the mall."

"But how does that fit with your lack of ambition and—"

"I thought you were going to shut up and listen."

He made his point. I waved my hand politely for him to continue.

"Thank you. Anyway, the girl who cut my hair was this hippy-type girl. She was older, mid-twenties I'd say. With wild, long hair and all this jewelry. She was also very...animated. I think she was high."

"You let some stoned, hippy chick come at you with scissors?"

He laughed. "I did. But first, she leaned my chair back and gave me a neck massage for some reason, which made my whole body go limp. Then she sat me up and never stopped talking the whole time she cut my hair, which she really screwed up by the way. But I didn't care; I was mesmerized. She practically danced around my chair the whole time."

"So, did the hippy chick help you decide what to major in or something?"

My dad laughed again. "Hardly. She invited me over to her apartment that night."

"Whoa. And you went?"

"Yep."

"Should we skip what happened at her apartment?"

"We can keep it PG-13, don't worry. The main thing is that she drugged me."

"She drugged you?"

"She did. I think she put something in a drink she made for me. Then we got into this whole existential, spiritual, hallucinogenic conversation about the meaning of life and my destiny. She was really big on destiny. The next thing I knew, it was morning. I woke up in her bed alone. Then some guy knocked on her bedroom door and told me to get out. I never saw her again."

I had no idea where to go with that. "OK, so…"

"The point is the whole experience left me questioning everything. Why was I in school? What was I going to do with my life? Why does Pia Zadora even exist?"

"Who is Pia Zadora?"

"That was a joke; you're too young. Never mind. The important thing is that I lost all motivation. And I dropped out of school at the end of that semester."

"Wow, Dad. I had no idea. What did your parents say?"

"Not much, surprisingly. They just said I was on my own as far as money goes. So, I got a job on campus, got an apartment, and just started practicing guitar and learning to sing along. After a few tries, I even landed my first gig at Greene Streets in Five Points. I used to hang out there a lot."

✌︎

After graduating from high school in 1981, Phillip enrolled as expected at the University of South Carolina in the tradition of his four siblings and his parents before him. But in the early fall of his sophomore year, a brief romantic encounter with a free-spirited, drug-using, twenty-six-year-old hairdresser unsettled Phillip's structured worldview. The chance meeting's hangover of influence left him inexplicably burdened with the question of life's purpose or, as she phrased it, his "destiny." Neither of which he had previously considered. Having had no discussions with his father or anyone else about why he was attending college or what he should be studying, Phillip began to experience a decline in academic motivation. Feeling time passing faster than his ability to absorb it, he dropped out of college after just three semesters.

Surprisingly, Phillip's parents expressed no opinions of his desire to slow down life's progress but simply informed him that in so doing he would assume full responsibility for his own financial needs. Having no desire to move back home to Charlotte, Phillip took a job in a drugstore near campus ringing up orders and cashing checks for university students, earning enough money to pay rent, if not much else, for a small apartment in Columbia.

Without the time demands of school or the social distractions of dorm life, Phillip focused on playing guitar. Living alone also afforded him the chance to sing along with his music, without fear of criticism or laughter. Gaining confidence, he began to consider playing for an audience. But his efforts to land a booking at any of a dozen local bars proved unsuccessful until Greene Streets, a small music venue near campus, accepted his offer to perform for free the next time they had a cancellation or an opening on their calendar. While waiting for that day to arrive, Phillip became a regular patron of the venue, as much as his small income would allow. It was there that he first met Gina.

ϟ

"So, random question," I said, "why did students cash checks at your drugstore?"

"This was before ATMs and debit cards," my dad explained. "If you needed cash and your bank wasn't open or in Columbia, you didn't have many options. We charged twenty-five cents to cash a check as long as you could show a student ID."

With a sly smirk, I asked, "Did you live in caves and wear animal skins, too?"

"You're really funny, Son."

"Sorry," I said, laughing at my own joke. "So, who was Gina?"

"Why don't we save that for next week? That's where it starts to hit the fan."

SIX

Gina

Despite the fact that my father has owned a coffee shop my whole life, I've never been much of a coffee drinker as far as volume and frequency go. When I was still in my teens, my dad taught me the ins and outs of coffee tasting. Not to brag, but I developed a very discriminating palate. The result being that I will only drink a cup of coffee if the flavor, body, and acidity meet my very specific taste preferences. I otherwise abstain. Which means I don't drink a lot of coffee. But when I am lucky enough to get a good cup in front of me, I do enjoy the experience. And since my father is the architect of my coffee snobbery, it was only natural that we meet in his café to continue working on our story. The Lost Bean is always a nice place to hang out, work, or socialize. Or talk with your dad about seeing a doctor for his memory issues. That was my plan, anyway.

When I arrived at the café shortly after seven o'clock that Wednesday evening, my father was already seated in one of the soft, leather chairs facing a round granite-top coffee table. "Hey, Dad," I said as I approached. I took a seat in the chair beside him.

"Hey, Son." He seemed a little stoic for some reason.

"Not very busy tonight," I said, looking around at the empty tables and chairs.

"That's summer for you. Fewer college students. Did you want something to drink before we get started? I've got a nice Nicaraguan you might like."

Before I could answer, one of my dad's employees stepped over to check on us.

"Hey, Mr. Johnson. How are you?"

"Hey, Julia. I'm fine. Julia, this is my son, Daniel."

"Oh, nice to finally meet you," said Julia.

I gave her a smile and a nod.

"Julia's a teacher, too, Daniel."

"Oh, cool," I said. "What do you teach?"

"Eleventh grade history over at Dreher."

"That's crazy; I teach tenth grade history at Heathwood."

"Ah, I've got you by a grade," she said, smiling. She then turned to my dad. "Can I get you and Daniel something?"

"If you could bring me a cup of our house coffee, black, and whatever he wants."

Hoping to avoid a potentially long coffee flavor discussion with my dad, I resisted temptation and asked Julia for a bottle of water.

"I'll be right back with those," she said, turning to leave.

"Water?" asked my dad.

"I'm thirsty," I said with a shrug. With Julia out of earshot, I asked, "She's worked for you a long time, hasn't she, Dad?"

"All through college and then four years after. Best employee I've ever had."

"Is she married?" I asked, stalling for time while I thought of how to bring up the doctor's visit.

"No," he said. "But she's got a thing for one of my regulars, though. They play chess together whenever he comes in. I think that's the only reason she still works here."

I paused for a moment, then decided to press forward. "So, how are you, Dad?"

"What do you mean?" he replied.

"Um, I'm just asking how you are."

"Son, I can tell the difference between a casual *how are you* and a probing *how are you*. That was a 'I'm concerned about my father' *how are you*."

I had to laugh at his insight. "OK, you caught me. I'm concerned about my dad. Nothing wrong with that, is there?"

"Let's don't start with all that tonight, please. I'm fine. I promise."

I'm ashamed to say I backed down quickly and opted to save the doctor conversation for later. "Well, good," I said, placing my phone on the table before us. "So, what did you want to talk about tonight?"

"I think it's time we jumped into Gina," he said.

"That sounds ominous."

He chuckled lightly. "You're not far off."

I tapped the record button on my phone's voice memos and asked, "OK, so who was Gina?"

"Well, honestly, when I met her, I thought I had found my…"

I thought I knew where he was going with that, so I tried to think of a description fitting for my dad's generation. "Soulmate?" I suggested.

"I wasn't going to say that."

"That's a relief."

"But something like that, yeah."

"Wow, Dad. Really?"

He paused for a moment as Julia placed our drinks on the coffee table then returned to the bar. "You have to understand," he said, "I had never met anyone like her. Gina was beautiful, glamorous, confident…"

"Like the hairdresser?"

My dad laughed. "No, thank goodness. Nothing like the hairdresser. Gina seemed to take a genuine interest in me and my music. Sparks flew and all that. But I had no way of knowing what I was getting myself into."

Gina Hazelton's enrollment at the University of South Carolina, a year before Phillip's arrival, had little to do with academics, a fact they held in common. But unlike Phillip's family expectation, Gina, a native New Yorker, had come south for the weather. While she would happily find a way to mention her family's summer home on Nantucket in almost any conversation, her winters growing up in Manhattan had been long and harsh.

The entertainment industry served as the overriding context for Gina's upbringing. Her father, Cole, a marketing executive for Warner Brothers Music, and her mother, Linda, a Broadway producer, were rarely available. As an only child accustomed to private school uniforms and the tutelage of nannies, Gina saw college as her first taste of freedom. And when choosing a school, the temperate climate of Columbia, South Carolina allowed for a much lighter wardrobe than her parents' choice of Princeton.

When Phillip's eyes found Gina from his corner barstool in Greene Streets that Tuesday night in late March 1983, her elegant beauty blinded him to the possibility of something less attractive lurking behind the green eyes smiling back at him.

"So, you met her at the music venue you told me about?"

"Yeah, I was there loitering at the bar, hoping the manager, Nick, would remember his promise to give me a chance on stage sometime."

"Had you written your own songs and everything?"

"Oh, gosh no. I took my brother's country records with me when I moved to my apartment in Columbia, so that's all I knew. I was anxious to see if I could really play in front of people. But that night, there was hardly anyone there. I guess that's why Nick told me to get up on stage."

"Had you already talked to Gina?"

"No, she had just come in. But I saw her across the bar. I was trying to get up the nerve to go talk to her when Nick came and got me."

"It's cool she happened to be there for your first show."

"It wasn't a coincidence."

∽◈∾

It was a slow night at Greene Streets, even for a Tuesday. Phillip sat alone quietly humming a melody, imagining his fingers moving across the frets of his guitar rather than the beer bottle in front of him. The music venue's stage and most of the tables facing it sat empty. As he rested on a stool at the back bar, he tried to see himself performing for the few people scattered around the room. It had been almost a month since he'd approached the venue's manager, Nick, about playing his first gig for free. Though Nick had given Phillip reason for hope, loitering in the bar several times a week as a visible reminder had yet to land him on stage.

In the few months since dropping out of school, Phillip had grown accustomed to being alone without the weight of loneliness. The friends he'd made during his time in school were still around, he assumed, but he held no connection to them. From the outside, college felt like a private country club to which he no longer claimed membership. He had climbed out of the pool, toweled off, and walked away. It felt good to be on his own. But he wasn't opposed to entertaining company, particularly if they looked like the girl standing across the bar from him.

Phillip tried to be discreet as he watched her wait for the bartender's attention. She leaned her elbows onto the bar, her gold earrings dancing in her long dark hair, and gave Phillip an inviting glance. He returned a quick smile but remained on his barstool. Looking toward the stage while he sipped his beer, he pondered what to say should he get the nerve to walk over. After finally just settling on "hello," he began to edge his way off his seat only to feel a hand on his shoulder. Phillip turned to see Nick, who, without small talk or explanation, offered him a chance to perform. While not grasping the immediacy of the offer, Phillip happily agreed.

"Great, you're on in five for thirty," said Nick, turning to walk away.

"You mean like now?" asked Phillip, slightly alarmed.

Nick simply gave a thumbs-up over his head as he left the bar area.

Forgetting about the girl, Phillip leapt from his barstool, ran to retrieve his guitar from his car trunk, then scurried back inside to the restroom where he made an intentional mess of his hair in front of the mirror. He gave himself a quick pep talk then turned to dry his hands.

"Ladies and gentlemen," Phillip heard over the whirl of the restroom hand dryer, "we have a surprise performance for you tonight." Phillip burst from the restroom, guitar in hand, and hurried toward the stage as Nick finished his introduction. "New to Greene Streets, please welcome Phillip Johnson."

As two or three patrons gave polite, if not hopeful, applause, Phillip climbed the stairs onto the stage. He stepped in front of the microphone and slipped the guitar strap over his head. The stage lights shining in his face made it difficult to see into the tiered seating area, but in the illumination of the back bar, he found his girl of interest offering her full attention. Phillip straightened the guitar against his stomach and, after clearing his throat and taking a deep breath, entered a brand-new world.

"I'd like to start with a song David Allan Coe did a couple years ago called *Tennessee Whiskey*," Phillip said as his heart pounded in his chest. He looked down at his hands in ready position and pleaded silently for them to cooperate. He then picked the intro's first few notes, strummed a perfect D chord, and began to sing.

Keeping his eyes closed as he sang, Phillip tried to pretend he was simply playing his guitar alone in his apartment. His nerves began to subside slightly as he lost himself in the tune. But as he finished the first verse, he opened his eyes to find the girl from the bar standing directly before the stage, staring up at him. Her surprise appearance and overt interest shot adrenaline through his body, disrupting his rhythm. He strummed his next chord down and up an extra time or two while gathering himself for the chorus. Looking down at her as he sang, her broad smile gave him the encouragement he sorely needed.

Phillip sang the rest of the song and the remainder of his set to his new and very first fan. And while Nick had given him thirty minutes to play, Phillip had no concept of time while he performed. After singing *Luckenbach, Texas* by Waylon Jennings, *Same Ole Me* by George Jones, *My Maria* by B.W. Stevenson, and *A Fire I Can't Put Out* by George Strait, he decided to close with his favorite Alabama song, *Feels So Right*. As Phillip locked eyes with the girl standing before him, the intimate lyrics seemed to echo what he already had in mind.

When he had finished, he thanked his audience over scattered applause, slid his guitar around behind him, and walked off stage to his left. Nick met him at the bottom of the stairs. He shook Phillip's hand and asked if he wanted to keep playing. Phillip looked at the girl waiting by the stage, prioritized his interests, and politely declined.

"Can you play anything besides country songs?" Nick asked.

"That's all I know, right now," replied Phillip, honestly.

"OK, here's the deal," said Nick, "We're always looking for good cover bands, and you've got talent. And the girls seem to dig you." He nodded toward the stage. "But you need a bigger sound. Get some guys to play with you, learn a few more songs – besides country – and I'll be happy to book you."

Phillip shook Nick's hand once more, said thank you, then turned his attention to the girl waiting patiently to meet him. She smiled as he approached.

"Hi," said Phillip.

"You were good up there," she said.

"Thanks. I appreciate you coming down front like that."

"Oh, I'm a big music fan," she gushed. "My family has a house on Nantucket, and we go to shows around there all summer long."

"What's your name?" he asked.

"Gina." She extended her hand toward him, her gold bracelets jingling around her thin wrist.

Phillip took hold of her hand, giving it a gentle squeeze as he studied her smile and glistening green eyes. "I'm Phillip," he said finally.

"Hi, Phillip."

"Hi, Gina," he said, a smile growing on his face. As a minor precaution, he added, "You're not a hairdresser, are you?"

"No," she laughed. "Why would you ask that?"

"Just making sure," he said, relieved. "Are you in school?"

"Yeah," she said, her eyes still locked on his. "I'm a junior in music industry."

"Music industry," Phillip repeated. "That's a major?"

"Sure. It's in the school of music. I want to be in the entertainment business. What are you studying?"

"Nothing at the moment; I'm taking a break."

"You're not in school?"

"Nope," said Phillip, ready to change the subject. "You want to grab a table?"

She smiled slyly and said, "I don't know if I can be seen with a college dropout."

Phillip took her flirting insult in stride. "Then how about a soon-to-be-famous musician?" he asked, raising an eyebrow.

"Now you're talking," said Gina.

৵৵

"So, what didn't go right with Gina? It sounds like you two really hit it off."

"We did, at first. But then there was the money problem. She had a lot of it. Her parents did, anyway. I barely had enough to feed myself. So, after we got past the initial attraction, I didn't have much to offer. I honestly didn't understand, at first, why she kept me around."

"Maybe she just liked you," I suggested. That made my dad laugh.

৵৵

When Phillip decided to leave school, his parents let him move his bedroom furniture from Charlotte to his small apartment in Columbia. A single-sized bed, nightstand, dresser, and desk were the only furnishings loaded into a rented

U-Haul truck, along with his brother's turntable and records. Having become acclimated to living in a college dorm, where a small bed served every purpose, the need for couches, chairs, love seats, rugs, tables, lamps, etc., never crossed Phillip's mind. Not that he could afford them if they did.

Gina's first visit to Phillip's apartment, just a day after they met, lasted less than two minutes. As he held the front door open, she stepped onto the bare hardwood floor of his empty den. The only visible sign that someone lived there was a small, rabbit-eared television set sitting on the fireplace hearth. Phillip preferred to have it in his bedroom, but the reception was better in the den. His offer to put towels on the floor if Gina wanted to watch TV failed to impress her. "Let's go to my place," she said.

Gina lived in a three-bedroom, fully furnished house her parents had purchased near campus her freshman year. Rather than paying rent or dormitory fees, her father saw Gina's college residence as an investment opportunity that would pay for itself when sold after her graduation. And it wasn't long before Phillip, while feeling somewhat out of place around Gina's two roommates, spent more time there than in his own apartment.

ઉ૰ન્ટ

"Why is that funny?" I asked. "You don't think she liked you?"

"I found out soon enough that people only mattered to Gina if they were useful to her. Take Nick, the manager I mentioned at Greene Streets. Gina and Nick were a couple before I came along. She'd been using him to find a band or a performer she could represent. She was in a hurry to try out her craft before she even finished college."

"Who told you that?"

"He did. That's why she was at Greene Streets the night I got on stage. When Nick saw me at the bar, he called her and told her to come down if she wanted to hear somebody new. And when she found me, she dumped Nick."

"So, I'm guessing she eventually did the same thing to you?"

"You're skipping way ahead," he said.

I watched his eyes wander around his café for a moment and waited for him to continue. "You want to keep going?" I finally asked.

My father reached for his coffee and said, "You know what? I think that's enough about Gina for one night. How about a game of chess?"

We moved to the community table where the chessboard sat ready to play. It had been a while since either of us had played, and I couldn't remember ever playing my dad. So, we kind of guessed at the rules. As we moved our pieces quietly across the board, it seemed like the perfect time to wade into the topic of him seeing a doctor.

"You know, I was talking to Elizabeth the other day," I said holding a white knight over the board.

"Don't you talk to her every day?" my father asked.

"Yeah, but…" I found a square for my knight and continued, "She was telling me about this kind of medicine you could take to prevent mini strokes."

My father moved his horse to a new square and said, "And you think I should be taking it, right?"

"Well, she is a nurse, Dad." I slid my castle a few squares forward.

My dad moved his queen across the board. "And she just randomly brought that up on her own?"

"Well, no. I…" I hadn't mentally prepared myself to get that far in the conversation and stalled for a moment. I pretended to be in thought about my next move, but my dad got tired of waiting.

"Daniel, I appreciate your concern. I really do. But I'm not ready to see a doctor just because I forget a few things every now and then. When I do make an appointment, it'll be my decision. Not yours or your mother's. Are you going to move or not?"

My chances of winning at chess were looking about as good as getting my dad to do something he didn't want to do. I considered my options and moved one of my pawns.

"Are you sure you want to do that?" he asked.

"Might as well."

He slid his knight toward my king and said, "Checkmate."

"That ended about like I thought it would," I said.

"The doctor discussion or the game?"

"Both."

SEVEN

Sleuthing

I spent the week following our time in the café typing up my notes and thinking about my dad's story. While my initial skepticism – actually, let's call it disbelief – remained, my father's recollection of his time growing up and in college seemed very authentic. I even Googled Gina Hazelton and found an obituary from ten years ago that seemed to match the girl we discussed. She passed away at age fifty-three from ovarian cancer that had spread to her lungs. Originally from New York, she'd been an executive with Universal Music Group in Los Angeles. She graduated from the University of South Carolina and never married or had kids. The discovery only made me more curious. I decided to approach my mother cautiously and see what, if anything, she knew.

To discreetly find time alone with my mom, I asked my dad when he was going to be in the café, the pretense being to get his help picking out a bag of coffee for Elizabeth. Once I got his schedule for a few days, I stopped by their house when I knew he would be gone. The excuse for my visit, as far as my mother was concerned, was to deliver a better birthday present to make up for the juicer. A blouse Elizabeth had picked out provided the perfect cover story. At some point during the visit, I had a feeling my mom would ask about my father's writing project. Once she did, I would have my opportunity to ask about Gina. After a few minutes of small talk, my mom did exactly as I expected.

"So, tell me about this story you and your father are working on," she said.

"Oh, we're just capturing some stories from his childhood, college, and his time playing guitar. That sort of thing."

"Kind of like a memoir?" she asked.

"I guess so, now that you mention it."

"Why all the secrecy, then? I already know all that stuff."

"I think he just wants to be sure it's a story worth sharing before he tells anyone about it."

"He's not repeating himself over and over again, is he?"

"No, actually his memory from years ago seems pretty clear. He may have told me a few minor things more than once, but he's doing fine. He remembers a lot of details and people's names, too. Like Nick, the manager of a music venue called Greene Streets. And he mentioned a girl he met there once. I think they dated." I pretended to think for a moment. "What was her name…"

"Was it Gina?"

"That's it," I said, pleased with my scheming. "Did you know her?"

"Not directly. But she had just broken up with your father right before I met him."

"Do you remember why she dumped him?"

"Well, don't say it like that."

"Why not?"

"It sounds bad."

"But she did, didn't she?"

My mom gave a conciliatory nod. "Yes, she did."

"How come?"

"Well…don't tell your father I told you this."

"It's our secret."

"OK. Well, Gina had her bigwig, music company father arrange a record label audition for your dad at a recording studio in Los Angeles."

"Wow, seriously? That's huge."

"It would have been if he had shown up for it."

"What do you mean?"

"He drove out there and got as far as New Mexico, but then he turned around and came home. When he got back to Columbia, she was so mad she broke up with him. I met him a couple of days later. We had coffee."

"You were his rebound girl?"

My mom laughed. "Yes, I suppose I was. But we made it last."

"I'll say. So did he tell you why he didn't go through with the audition?"

"Honestly, I've always wondered if he was just afraid he'd go out there and fail. He told me sometimes dreams are better than reality. And he'd rather just keep his dreams."

"Ah, the 'just dreams' comment."

"Yep. But don't you dare tell him I told you all that."

"I promise, Mom."

"And thank you so much for my blouse. Please tell Elizabeth I said thank you."

"It's that obvious?"

"Just a bit," she said with a wink.

"Well," I said, "she has nice taste."

My mom patted me on the shoulder. "In clothes *and* men," she said.

"Thanks, Mom."

EIGHT

The Sole Winners

With confirmation that Gina was a real person in my dad's life, it became clear that his storytelling seemed to oscillate between truth, exaggeration, and fiction. If we were looking to write a novel, that wouldn't be a bad approach. But his insistence on its truth in whole cast a shadow over an otherwise fun exercise. And how much of that shadow stemmed from a medical issue remained a concern. When we met at my house the next Wednesday, I tried to steer our discussion toward what I knew to be true, at least in part. My mom said he was in a band. I started there.

"So, Dad," I said as we took our seats in my den. "I'm anxious to hear more about the Bread Winners."

"I think you mean Sole Winners," he said, scratching Bono's back.

"What did I say?"

"Bread Winners."

"Oh, sorry. Sole Winners. Anyway, do you want to talk about how you guys got started and all that? Where did y'all play?"

"Before we get into the band, there's one more girl that's part of the story."

"Another one?"

"Yep. We haven't talked about Vallie."

"Valley," I repeated, writing her name on my notepad.

"That's Vallie with an 'ie' at the end," he said.

"Vallie. Got it. Who was she?"

"Well, for one thing, she wasn't from New York. She grew up about an hour from here in Manning."

"Small town girl," I said.

"She was, but she didn't want to stay that way like her two older sisters. The first time I saw Vallie I was working in the drugstore that August, my first summer since dropping out of school. All the students had just come back into town for fall semester, and she came in with a friend. I remember, once she came in the door I couldn't take my eyes off her."

"So, was this after you dated Gina?"

"No, we were still dating. We'd been together a few months by that time, over that summer."

I grinned at my father. "But you had eyes for Vallie?"

"Well, I couldn't help it; she was really pretty."

My grin gave way to a laugh.

"Why is that so funny?" he asked.

"I'm sorry," I said. "I guess it's just that hearing your dad was a sucker for a pretty face is kind of refreshing in a way."

"I was young once too, you know."

"I know, sorry. So, go ahead. She was good-looking."

"She was. But in a different way from Gina. She wasn't wearing any makeup and just had long, straight, blonde hair. She had this natural, wholesome thing going on. Gina was always so put together, with the makeup and lipstick and hair and everything. Besides, things weren't really going so well for me with Gina around that time."

"Why? I thought she was your soulmate."

"I did not say that; you did."

"You're right," I conceded. "So, what went wrong?"

"She made me feel like I worked for her. Like she owned me or something. Which in a way was my fault."

"Why didn't you just break up with her."

"It wasn't that simple. I was trapped. She made everything happen as far as the band goes. Where we played, what we played. If the guys had an issue or question, they went to her, not me. And then there was something else I haven't even told you about yet." My dad paused for a moment.

I wondered if he was referring to his aborted audition in L.A., but I kept my promise to my mother and said nothing.

"But, man," he continued, "when I saw Vallie that day in the store…she was all I could think about afterward."

"When did you see her again?"

"Not for a few months, but I looked for her all the time. I was able to get introduced to her one night that November. She was already dating some guy in Charleston, but I knew right then, she was my…"

I smiled at my dad. "Do you want to say it this time?"

"Very funny. I was going to say, 'my destiny', but that sounds worse than soulmate."

ॐ

In late August of that year, Phillip took note of an attractive blonde meandering around his drugstore with a friend, laughing as they paused to sort through a display of cheap sunglasses. His wish that she would come to his register was granted when she placed a personal check and student ID on the counter before him. The name printed on the check to be cashed read Valerie Ray. The soft smile and blue eyes captured in her ID matched those waiting patiently before him. After exchanging transactional pleasantries, she was gone. But in the days and months that followed, a hopeful expectation that she may return filled Phillip's mind.

A junior at the university studying education, Valerie – or "Vallie" to her friends – had grown up an hour away from

Columbia in a town called Manning. Her two older sisters, identical twins who dominated attention at any social gathering, had already earned their college degrees and returned home, settling for small-town lives dating old boyfriends from high school and working in their father's furniture store. Vallie wanted more. Her storybook views on life and love filtered any relationship, the latest involving a boy attending the College of Charleston. But despite his romantic appeals, those idealistic dreams kept her from committing. She wasn't sure if he was The One.

Vallie and Gina couldn't have been more different. But that night in November when Phillip finally looked again into those blue eyes and said, "It's nice to meet you, Vallie," he knew he had found his "destiny."

ॐ

"OK, any more about Vallie?" I asked.

"Yeah, but we'll come back to her later. Let's talk about the band for a few minutes."

"Oh, good. How did that get started? You went from just playing by yourself to having your own band."

"Well, Gina was the driving force behind all that. I came over to her house one night for a party she was throwing, and she introduced me to my band."

"Just like that?"

"Just like that."

ॐ

In the weeks following his performance at Greene Streets, Phillip used his spare time to learn new songs from a handwritten list of suggestions provided by Gina, along with a stack of her cassette tapes and records. Top 40 pop-rock songs like *Jack and Diane* by John Cougar, *867-5309* by Tommy

Tutone, and *Every Breath You Take* by the Police. The songs were easy enough to play and sing, but he wasn't sure what to do about Nick's requirement to form a band. Phillip didn't know any other musicians. But Gina had quietly taken that task in hand.

Leveraging her school of music contacts and friends around campus, Gina spread the word about a new cover band in need of members. Without consulting Phillip, she christened the band the Sole Winners, a subtle pun aimed at the Bible Belt. Making use of her persuasive charm and confident promotion of Phillip's talent, she secured a bass player, a drummer, and an electric guitarist who were all interested and willing to join the band.

Following spring semester final exams, Gina threw a large party at her house. When Phillip arrived after his closing shift at the drugstore, he could hear music and voices from Gina's house a block away. Given the number of cars parked up and down the street, Phillip wondered if he would know anyone there besides Gina. Once inside, he meandered through the crowd toward the kitchen in the rear of the house. There he found Gina, beer in hand, laughing with three boys he'd never seen before. She spotted him before he had a chance to say hello.

"Oh, there he is!" she shouted, waving Phillip over. "Get over here; I have a surprise for you."

Phillip joined Gina at the kitchen center island, put his arm around her thin waist, and kissed her. "Hey," he said.

"Are you ready?" she asked, clearly excited and slightly drunk.

"Ready for what?"

"Guys, come over here," she said, pulling the three boys closer. "Phillip, this is Michael Lane. He's a percussionist from..." She looked to Michael.

"Maryland," he said.

She continued, "Majoring in music performance. And this is Zack Flynn. He's from right here in Columbia, and he plays electric guitar. And this is Braden LeClair, your bass player from Chicago."

"Madison, Wisconsin," corrected Braden.

"And the best part is," gushed Gina, "they're all going to be around Columbia this summer, so you can start playing!"

"I'm sorry, I guess I'm missing something," said Phillip.

"This is your band, silly! The Sole Winners!"

"My band? But I..."

"I did this for you! And I've already got you guys booked at Greene Streets in three weeks!"

"Wait, the *Soul* Winners?" asked Phillip. "You mean like Billy Graham or something?"

Gina laughed. "No, like the *only* winners. The Sole Winners! It's just a little pun."

"That might get confusing," said Phillip.

"That's what I said," offered Braden.

"Guys, it's on purpose," argued Gina. "It'll get people talking. Trust me; I know these things."

≫≪

"So, how long did y'all play together as a band, Dad?" I asked.

"Just a few months. We played gigs around town through the summer and then a lot when fall semester started." He paused for a moment, then said, "Son, why don't we stop there for tonight."

I studied my dad's face. He suddenly looked older for some reason. "Are you all right, Dad? You're looking a little tired."

"I'm fine," he said, rubbing his forehead. "I'm just feeling a little woozy for some reason."

"Can I get you something to drink?"

"Just some water would be good."

I hurried into the kitchen and returned with a glass of water.

"Thank you," he said. After taking a couple of sips, he said, "Daniel, I realize the things I'm telling you aren't normal father-son topics. Girls and college parties and things like that."

"It's OK, Dad. I appreciate you sharing all this with me."

"I have to say, talking about Gina is bringing back some bad memories, and if I seem a bit tired, that's probably why. It's just a little taxing."

"We can just keep it at a high level if you want to," I offered. "Besides, the story's about you, not her. By the way, I wasn't going to mention this, but I saw an obituary online for a Gina Hazelton, and I wondered if it might be her."

My father nodded his head. "I heard she passed away about ten years ago, I think."

"Yep," I said. "Of cancer. It said she worked in the music industry in Los Angeles and that she never married."

"Well, technically," he said, "that's not entirely accurate."

"Which part?"

"Her not being married."

"How do you know that?"

"Because she was married to me at one point."

I'd like to say I handled that revelation with the same cavalier, enabler attitude I'd maintained over our previous few discussions. But this time, I dropped my head into my hands.

My dad gave me a moment to gather myself.

I lifted my head, sighed, and asked with resignation, "So, you were married to Gina before Mom?" I already knew the answer to that question was no.

"It wasn't before your mom; it was instead of."

It was the same "instead of" comment he made about me. "You mean the whole, time travel thing again?"

His expression suddenly changed as if he'd remembered something. "You know, Gina passed away about ten years ago."

My heart sank as I looked at him. "Why don't we just call it a night, Dad."

NINE

Santa Rosa

After my father left, I called Elizabeth for our usual end-of-the-day chat. When I told her how my father had mentally faded at the end of our discussion, she scolded me. She was unhappy that I had let him drive home by himself. I should have at least followed him, she said, to make sure he didn't get lost. While I appreciated her concern, I honestly didn't believe he could get lost driving to his own house. He wasn't an amnesia patient, I thought. I didn't say that, of course. But, just to cover my bases, I sent him an innocuous text message to be sure he'd made it home safely.

> Hey Dad, I think I left my sunglasses in your den last time I was there. Could you take a look?
>
> I looked but didn't see them.
>
> OK. Thanks. Goodnight.
>
> Night.

I let Elizabeth know he had made it home. But her concern made me wonder if I was still in denial over the serious nature of his mental condition. She was a nurse, after all, and I wasn't. I resolved to be more aware going forward.

Our next meeting was back at his house, so there was no worry about him driving. I hadn't eaten before leaving, so I made a quick stop at Firehouse Subs on the way. Once at my dad's house, I settled in at the kitchen table and ate while I recorded his story. To help us get started, and to avoid repetition, I gave him a quick synopsis of our last discussion.

"That was helpful," he said. "I think I might have mentioned last week that there was one thing about Gina I hadn't told you."

I did remember him saying that, but I was thankful he did too. "OK," I said, "what is it?"

"It's really the big thing," he said.

"I'm ready; just hit me with it." I took a bite of my turkey sub sandwich and prepared myself for another surprise.

"When you asked last week why I didn't break up with Gina, I said because I felt trapped."

"That's right."

"Well, here's why. Gina was always bragging about how she could get her dad to do anything she wanted. I'd listen to her on the phone with him sometimes, and she'd smile at me and wiggle her pinky finger."

"Like he was wrapped around it or something?"

"Exactly. So, after our band started playing bars in Columbia that summer and getting some buzz around town, she convinced her father to arrange an audition for me with one of his company's record labels out in Los Angeles."

I stopped myself from saying, "You mean the audition you didn't go to." But instead, I asked, "For you or the whole band?"

"Just me. But I had to wait until November to go out there. So, basically, for the three months leading up to it, she controlled any hope I had of a music career."

"She really did own you."

"She did. I was even sure she was cheating on me with our drummer, Michael. But there was nothing I could do about it."

ço∾

Heading into her senior year of college, Gina's career ambitions couldn't wait for graduation. To compensate for her teenage decision to attend a university in southern fly-over country, she aggressively applied a New Yorker's mindset to the Columbia live music scene. Finding marketable talent was step one. Learning to manage and promote her product was step two. As such, her interest in Phillip had little to do with him, personally. He was simply a training opportunity, a small step on a ladder, a long-shot lottery ticket. And while Phillip held on to the idea that he was in some form of romantic relationship with Gina, he slowly came to accept the cage in which he lived. He was captive to his own hopes and dreams. And Gina held the key.

ço∾

"I'm starting to see why you took an interest in Vallie when she came into your store."

My father nodded his head. "She looked like everything Gina wasn't. And when I saw her, I thought, 'That's what I want. Someone like that.'"

I could empathize. "I think everyone's done that at least once or twice."

"What's that?"

"You know, fill in the blanks around someone's looks just to suit your own needs. A girl's pretty so we think she'll be whatever we want her to be. But it doesn't always work out that way."

"Since when did my son get so wise in the ways of women?"

"Elizabeth keeps me honest."

"You need to marry that girl."

I was quick to get us back on topic. "Anyway, what were you saying?"

"Oh. Um…"

"You thought Vallie was cute so she must be the perfect girl for you."

"You've made your point."

"Sorry, so what about the audition, then? How did that go?" I was still hoping his story would match what my mother had already told me. But of course, it didn't.

"Let's just say I didn't wow them the first time."

"The first time? You mean you had more than one audition?"

"This is where things start to get a little…messy."

"That's all right. Let's go," I said, ready for anything.

"Well, first I had to drive out to Los Angeles for the audition. I had no idea how long it would take, so I gave myself a few days to get out there."

"Why didn't you just fly?"

"I couldn't afford it, and I didn't want Gina paying for it. She had enough leverage over me, already. I wanted to do it myself."

"So how long did it take you?"

"Five days."

"Five? Which way did you go?"

"Before I left, I bought a map of all fifty states and got a blue highlighter and marked a route up to Asheville to I-40 west through Oklahoma and the Texas panhandle and on out to L.A. But I got stuck on the way out there in a little town called Santa Rosa, New Mexico."

"Never heard of it."

"I hadn't neither. But by the second night of driving, I was pretty tired. I was out in the desert about an hour west of

Amarillo, and there weren't any exits for miles and miles. It was late, so I just pulled over and went to sleep. When I woke up the next morning, my car wouldn't start."

"Dead battery?"

"That's what I assumed, but it turned out to be a bad starter."

"Wait a minute," I said, putting down my sandwich. "Didn't something like that happen to a character in one of your books?"

"Yep, in my first novel. Like they say, write what you know."

"I thought that sounded familiar," I said, still wondering if we were talking about fact or fiction.

"Anyway, this was way before cell phones so when I woke up the next morning, I just sat on the trunk of my car and waited for someone to come by. It was five in the morning, so it took about an hour. Finally, this old couple in a van from Michigan stopped and gave me a lift. They were on one of those *See America* trips across the country. I think the only reason the man picked me up was to have someone to talk to. His wife was sound asleep. The next exit was Santa Rosa an hour up the road, so I just listened to him all the way there."

"How big is Santa Rosa?"

"I'm sure it's all built up now, but back then it was just an exit loop with a big truck stop. Other than a cheap motel across the street and an old bar next to it, I don't remember much else around there. But the truck stop had a mechanic's garage, and once they opened, they sent a tow truck out to get my car. I had nothing to do for a while, so around noon I wandered across the street to the bar."

"Uh-oh," I said, grinning. "I sense a plot development."

"I guess you could say that. In the bar, I met these two Indian women–"

"You mean Native American?"

"Yes, sorry, Native American. They were Apache. I started talking to them, and they ended up driving me out into the desert to show me a couple natural wonders."

"Wait, first the hairdresser and now you just go out in the desert with two strange women you met in a bar? What the heck, Dad?"

"I know; it sounds bad. And I even wondered the whole time if they were just going to kill me and leave my body out there for the buzzards to eat."

I shook my head at my dad's youthful lack of discretion. "You know, most people would think about that first and then not go."

"Well, they were very persuasive. And a little mysterious. Besides, I had downed a few beers. And a shot, so…"

♀◦♂

When Phillip opened the bar's screened door, he only saw three people inside: two Native American women on stools facing a man behind the bar. All three turned their attention to Phillip. The lack of music and the door's creaking springs made his slow entrance even more awkward.

"Come on in," the bartender finally said with a wave of his hand. "Have a seat." He gestured to a stool next to the women.

"What can I get you?"

"I'll have a Miller Lite," Phillip said, settling onto the bar stool.

"We have Budweiser," said the bartender.

"Bud Light?"

"Budweiser."

"That'll work, thanks."

"Hello," said the woman seated farthest from Phillip. "What's your name?"

"Phillip."

"You can tell a lot about someone from their name," she said.

The bartender popped the cap off Phillip's Budweiser and set the cold, wet bottle in front of him.

Phillip thanked the bartender then said to the woman, "I'm pretty sure Phillip's just a random white kid name."

"You see?" she said, smiling. "I just learned that you're a random white kid."

The bartender laughed as he wiped the counter.

"I'm called Gouyen," she said, "and this is my sister Bina."

Phillip took a much-needed swig from his beer. "Nice to meet you," he said, wiping his sweatshirt sleeve across his mouth.

"Do you play music?" asked Bina.

"Um, I do," Phillip said, caught off guard by the question. "I play guitar. What made you ask that?"

"I could just tell," said Bina. "I play flute."

Gouyen sat with her elbows on the bar studying Phillip's face. "You look sad," she said.

"Oh, my car broke down out in the desert last night," he explained. "I'm having it towed in."

"That's not it," said Gouyen. "You have a woman, don't you?"

"Well, yeah," Phillip said, feeling a little intruded upon. "I've got a girlfriend. Why?"

"What's her name?"

"It's Gina."

"Is Gina nice to you?" asked Gouyen.

Phillip thought about the question for a moment. "Well, I don't know if nice is the right word. She does nice things for me, but they're usually for her, too, so…"

"She's been unfaithful to you, hasn't she?" asked Gouyen.

The question was alarmingly insightful, given Gina's trysts with Michael. "Why would you ask that?"

"Because your spirit is that of a prisoner. A man who longs for another life."

The bartender jumped in. "I should warn you," he said to Phillip. "You're outmatched with these two. Be careful."

Phillip gave him a nod, then turned to Gouyen. "I'm nobody's prisoner," he said, though it felt like a lie. "I promise."

"Maybe you're a prisoner of your own fate," said Gouyen, "and you just don't know it."

Phillip scowled at Gouyen. "And you do?"

The bartender placed a shot of whiskey in front of Phillip. "Here, it's on me. You'll thank me later."

Phillip laughed. "Thanks, man." He threw the shot down his throat, shook his head, and asked, "So, my own fate, huh? Isn't fate kind of non-negotiable? Like destiny?"

"You can choose your own destiny," said Gouyen.

Phillip couldn't ignore the feeling of déjà vu. "So, I have to ask, do you two work around here?"

"We both work at the hair salon down the street," said Bina.

Phillip laughed heartily. "You're hairdressers?"

Gouyen and Bina nodded.

Shaking his head, Phillip said, "This all makes perfect sense now." He tilted his beer against his lips for a long moment, swallowed, and decided to humor his new friends. "So, I'm curious. Just how would I go about choosing my own fate?"

"We can show you if you like," said Gouyen.

"Ladies," said the bartender, "maybe you should leave the kid alone. Remember what happened the last time?"

While Phillip appreciated the bartender's concern, he didn't like being referred to as a kid. "No, I've got this," he said. "It's OK." He turned to the ladies. "We're just having fun, right?" Phillip tapped the top of his empty beer bottle. The bartender took the cue and placed another Budweiser in front of him.

"The question you need to ask is," said Gouyen, "'What would I do with a second chance?'"

"A second chance at what?"

"That's for you to decide," said Gouyen.

"I'm sorry, but you're not making much sense," Phillip said. He took a long swig from his beer and said, "I'd better go check on my car."

"You can't leave," said Gouyen. "We have things to do."

"We do?" asked Phillip, sarcastically.

"Come with us," she said, grabbing her keys off the bar.

"Where are we going?"

"You can't visit Santa Rosa without seeing the sights."

Phillip laughed. "I've already seen the truck stop and the bar. What else is there?"

"You've only seen what man has made. There's more. Come."

Ignoring his better judgment, and for lack of anything else to do, Phillip grabbed his beer and hopped off his bar stool. After paying his tab, he followed the women out of the bar and climbed into the back of Gouyen's small car. A short drive later, they arrived at what the locals called Blue Hole. Phillip got out of the car and followed his new friends down a dirt path around a group of tall boulders.

Stopping before a large pool of clear, blue water, Gouyen asked, "Well, what do you think?"

"It's a pool of water," said Phillip, unimpressed.

"It's Blue Hole. It's a gift of Nature. See that dark space way down there at the bottom? That's a cave entrance. It winds down into the earth. No one knows how deep it is. People have gone scuba diving into it and never come back."

"You mean there are dead bodies floating around down there somewhere?"

Gouyen nodded, "Their spirits now guard the entrance."

Phillip pointed to a *Swim at Your Own Risk* sign on one of the large rocks above the pool. "Did their spirits put up that sign, too?" he asked with a mocking chuckle.

"You don't believe in spirits?" asked Gouyen.

Phillip held up his bottle of beer as if he were making a toast. "I believe in Jim Beam and Budweiser. How about that?"

Gouyen turned to Bina and said something in a language Phillip had never heard before. Bina responded in the same tongue but seemed to disagree with her sister. Whatever they were discussing, Gouyen seemed to prevail. She turned to Phillip. "We're going to show you something else."

෨෮

After listening to my dad's memories of the two ladies in Santa Rosa and laughing along with him for close to an hour, I noticed him starting to look tired. Not as bad as the last time, but Elizabeth's scolding was still fresh in my mind. Rather than showing worry, or quoting my girlfriend again, I decided to just make it about me.

"Hey Dad, do you mind if we stop there for tonight? I promised Elizabeth I'd swing by her place."

"Sure, that's fine, Son. Your mom will be getting home soon, anyway."

"Cool. This was fun tonight. And by the way, I think I've figured out why you learned to cut your own hair."

"It's cheaper and safer," my dad said with a smile.

TEN

Black Hole

I really did stop by Elizabeth's house that Wednesday evening. But despite what I had told my father, she wasn't expecting me. I thought it would be fun to surprise her. As it turned out, she surprised me. After welcoming me in, she asked me to have a seat in her den and proceeded to tell me she wanted us to "take a break." It took a few clarifying questions for me to realize she was breaking up with me. She wasn't sure where our relationship was headed, that sort of thing. But she still wanted us to be friends. Of course. I like to think I handled it well, but I decided not to call or text her for at least a week. I was curious to see if she really wanted to keep me as a friend, so I left it up to her to reach out. By the time I met with my dad a week later, I still hadn't heard from her.

My dad wanted to meet at my place again. The women's church group was gathering at their house that night, so he needed an escape plan anyway. He arrived shortly after seven o'clock.

I hadn't told my parents the Elizabeth news to avoid hearing "I told you so" over and over again. I wanted to keep it quiet as long as possible and had no plans to discuss it with my dad. He rang the front doorbell as usual and came in after I yelled from the kitchen. The first thing he said to me was, "What's this I hear about you and Elizabeth breaking up?"

"Dad, seriously? Who told you that?"

"Your mother, of course. They talk, you know that."

I pressed my lips together to keep the expletives locked inside my head.

"We tried to tell you," he said. "You should've married that girl while you had the chance."

"Dad, I really don't want to talk about it, OK? We're just taking a break. That's all."

"Uh-huh. A break."

"Give it a rest, please, Dad? I'm going to try and fix it. I just need some time."

"You're not getting any younger, Son."

"Thanks for that, Dad. Can we just drop it and talk about your story tonight?"

"That's fine. Just let me know if I can help in any way with Elizabeth."

That was the second time he'd made that offer, but I still had no idea what he meant by it.

"Have a seat," I said, motioning to the kitchen table. I grabbed my phone and began recording. With a large, cleansing sigh, I said, "So. Where were we?"

"Santa Rosa."

"Oh, that's right. Santa Rosa. Those two women took you out to Blue Hole."

I was thankful I was recording our conversation because it took me a few minutes to focus on what my dad was saying. Elizabeth was occupying more space in my head than she did before she broke up with me. But slowly, I disconnected from my circumstances and began listening to my father's story.

"After we left Blue Hole," he said, "Gouyen drove us north under I-40 on Highway 91 and onto this dirt road that took us out into the desert. We bounced along for a good ten or fifteen minutes. It wasn't like a regular road that people drove on. Bina called it a horse trail."

"Is this when you wondered if they were going to feed you to the buzzards?" I asked.

My dad laughed. "That's exactly what I was wondering at the time. Especially when she stopped the car with nothing around."

༄༅

The car stopped. Phillip looked in all directions but saw nothing but desert terrain; they were truly in the middle of nowhere. As Gouyen and Bina climbed out, Phillip sat motionless in the backseat, unsure what was about to happen. Gouyen knocked on the window and motioned for him to follow. After a moment's hesitation, he shrugged off his fears and joined them.

The two women led Phillip on a trail through a group of trees that ended at the edge of a small canyon. A clear, shallow river flowed slowly below.

"That's the Pecos River," said Bina.

"Have a seat," said Gouyen, as she sat down on a boulder overlooking the canyon.

"So, what's the big attraction here?" Phillip asked, sitting down next to Gouyen.

Gouyen pointed to the other side of the canyon. "Do you see that?"

"See what?" asked Phillip.

"Across the river. The dark shadow at the bottom of the hill."

"Sure, what about it?"

"That holds the answer to your question."

"What question?"

Gouyen kept her gaze across the river. "Once upon a time, there was a great flood. The first—"

"Is Noah's ark down there?" interjected Phillip, enjoying himself.

Gouyen ignored him. "The first woman, Esdzanadehe, who we call White Painted Woman, survived the rising waters by hiding in an abalone shell. After the flood had passed, she climbed to the top of a great mountain. There she was given a child by the Sun. The child became Killer of Enemies. The Rain gave her a second child, Son of Water. Together, they defeated the Dark Ones and made the earth safe for all mankind."

"OK, so...," mused Phillip.

"Across this river is Black Hole," continued Gouyen, pointing to the dark shadow. "Its entrance faces the new day sun. As White Painted Woman grows old, she walks east toward the rising sun and into the past. She then becomes young again. You can do the same if you choose to."

Bina jumped in with a sense of urgency. "Phillip, she doesn't speak for our people! Don't listen—"

"Be quiet!" shouted Gouyen. "He must decide."

"Decide what?" asked Phillip. "What are we even talking about here?"

"Black Hole," Gouyen said reverently. "Is there a younger time you would return to, if you could, and do things differently?"

"Well, right now I'm wishing I would have just waited in the truck stop instead of going to the bar."

"You joke," said Gouyen. "What I speak of is real. It's there waiting for you. Enter Black Hole before the sun rises. Walk a straight path into the darkness. And emerge with the rising sun to a younger day."

"Wait a sec," said Phillip. "Are you talking about going back in time? Seriously?"

"Whether you believe it or not, doesn't change the truth."

❦

"Wait a minute," I said to my dad, "I've heard you say that *believe it or not* thing before."

"Now you know where I got it from," he said.

"You really talked to these ladies?"

"I've told you; I'm not making this stuff up. But, again, if it makes you feel better, just think of it as a story your crazy old dad is telling you."

I didn't know which way I was leaning on that point. The details of my father's story – and the way he told it – hardly seemed like fabrication. But I knew the specter of time travel still loomed ahead. "So, is this where you traveled back in time?" I asked. "Did you go back and dump Gina? Or ask out Vallie when she came in the store?"

"Woah, slow down. No, I didn't go in Black Hole then. I pretty much dismissed everything Gouyen said as spiritual fantasy and myths."

"Ah, you said *pretty much*. Does that mean you left some room to wonder about what she was saying?"

"It's fair to say that. After they took me back to the truck stop, I went in to check on my car. The manager said it would be ready the next morning, so I stayed in a five-dollar-a-night motel room across the street."

"Five dollars? What year was this, again?"

"1983. My room had one single-sized bed, a broken air conditioner in the window, and no hot water. So, yeah, five dollars."

❦

When Phillip picked up his car the next morning, the mechanic who made the repairs met him at the payment counter. The name in the white oval on his chest pocket read "Nitis." He seemed to be of the same heritage as Gouyen and Bina, so while Phillip paid his bill, he quizzed Nitis. "Question for you," Phillip said. "Have you ever heard of Black Hole?"

Nitis gave Phillip a quizzical look and asked, "Don't you mean Blue Hole?"

"No, Black Hole. It's out in the desert on the Pecos River."

Nitis looked down for a minute to focus on the repair paperwork. Without looking up at Phillip, he said, "It sounds like you've been talking to Gouyen."

"You know her?"

"Yes, I know Gouyen."

"Was she telling me the truth about Black Hole?"

Nitis handed Phillip his credit card. "I'll only say this: Just because her name means *wise woman*, doesn't mean she knows what she's talking about. And what she says about Black Hole sounds Apache, but it's not. Besides, the last guy she took out there got bit by a rattlesnake. If I were you, I'd just be on my way and forget about Gouyen and Black Hole."

৶৹৶

"So, one more question before we stop for tonight," I said. "Did you keep going to L.A. or come back home?"

I was hoping he'd stay with me in reality, but instead, he said, "I was in Los Angeles twelve hours later."

ELEVEN

Cat & Mouse

The next week went by slowly. It had been two weeks since Elizabeth and I started our "break," and I still hadn't heard from her. Perhaps even more odd was the fact that my mother hadn't called me either. I fully expected to be harassed for my failure to give her the daughter-in-law she always wanted. But as of that Wednesday, not a word.

My mom sent me a text message that morning, asking if I could come over to the house after lunch while my father was at the café. She didn't give a reason, but I assumed she was finally ready to give me an earful. I planned to just make an afternoon of it and hang around until my dad got home. We could then decide where to continue working on our story.

When I arrived, my mom was seated at the kitchen table with a glass of iced tea, reading the paper as I entered through the garage. She got up, gave me a hug, and we exchanged pleasantries. Once we sat down, she jumped right into her reason for asking me over.

"Your father has had a rough week," she said.

It wasn't the topic I was expecting, but I rolled with it and asked, "What happened?"

"Well, first, last Friday he couldn't remember what he did with the checkbook. We looked all over for it, and I finally found it in his car above the sun visor. He must have left it there after he went to the bank."

"That could happen to anyone, Mom."

"But then I was telling him about my friend Lucy from church – she's having an operation next week – and he had no idea who I was talking about. He's met her a hundred times."

I raised an eyebrow. "A hundred times, really?"

"OK, he's met her a lot, but–"

"Did he tell you he didn't know her?"

"No, he faked it for a minute or two, but I could tell by the blank look on his face he was lost. When I asked him if he knew who I was talking about he lied and said he did. So, I pressed him on it, and he had to admit that he was drawing a blank. When I showed him her picture on Facebook of course he knew who she was." My mom shook her head, then drank the last of her tea. "And then, I took Pumpkin to the vet yesterday, and she's gained ten pounds."

I was trying to follow. "And…are we still talking about Dad?" I asked.

"Yes, we're still talking about your dad. Twice this week, he forgot that he'd already fed Pumpkin, and I caught him trying to feed her again. I think he's been doing that a lot. Of course, Pumpkin doesn't mind; she thinks it's great. More food for her."

My laughter wasn't the reaction my mom was hoping for.

"Daniel, I need you to talk to him again about seeing his doctor."

"Mom, I've tried several times. He's very adamant about it. He wants it to be his decision, not something he's forced to do."

"Well, I honestly don't know what to do with him." She got up from the table and placed her empty glass in the sink. "How's he doing with your little writing project?"

I rose from the table and leaned against the counter. "He's still doing well with it, mostly. The amount of detail he remembers–"

"Your father has quite an imagination, you know."

"I know, but still. Even when he talks about the stuff I know didn't really happen, he makes it seem like a genuine experience. I just–"

"Like what stuff?"

"Whoops. I'm not supposed to share any details. Sorry."

My mother shook her head in frustration. "I still don't understand why y'all are being so secretive. He won't tell me anything about it, either. It makes me wonder if he just can't remember what he's telling you."

"Well, we are recording all our sessions," I said.

A light bulb appeared above my mother's head. "Was recording his idea or yours?" she asked.

"It was his," I said. "He thought it would help me when I write about what we discuss."

"Uh-huh," she said knowingly. "Have you considered that he may want you to record it because he's afraid he'll forget what he's told you?"

She had a legitimate point. "I hadn't thought of it like that."

"Just promise me you'll talk to him again. Please, Son?"

"OK," I conceded. "I'll try." And in an attempt to get my break-up lecture over with, I added, "And Mom, about Elizabeth–"

She gave a wave of her hand as she turned back toward the sink. "That's really none of my business," she said.

"Seriously?" I said with a laugh. "Since when is my relationship with Elizabeth none of your business?"

She breezed past me to the table and began folding up the newspaper. "Daniel, you and Elizabeth are adults. I'm sure you're doing whatever you feel is best."

"Mom, did you fall and hit your head or something? Maybe I should take *you* to the doctor instead of Dad."

"Don't be silly," she said. She put a congenial smile on her face and said, "I didn't offer you anything to drink; would you like some iced tea?"

As I stood there with my mouth hanging open, I realized something was definitely amiss.

TWELVE

Hollywood

The confusing spin my mother put on my break-up situation was enough to make me go home rather than hang around their house all afternoon. But on the way, I decided to stop by the Lost Bean to see if I could catch my dad. Since I had my laptop with me, I hoped we could work on the story there for a little while. If nothing else, I could use a distraction from the constant temptation to text Elizabeth. I found him sitting at the large community table typing on his laptop. I snuck up behind him and said, "How's the coffee here?"

"Well, hey, Son," he said, twisting around on his stool. "I'm surprised to see you."

I took a seat next to him. "Mom said I might find you here. I stopped by the house to see her for a few minutes earlier."

"That was brave of you," he said, with a grin.

"If you mean the whole Elizabeth thing, believe it or not, she didn't want to talk about it. It was really weird."

"Hmm…She hasn't said much to me about it either, now that I think about it. Maybe she's just finally learned to stay out of your love life."

"Yeah, right," I said with a laugh. "Anyway, I was wondering if we could work on your story some here instead of waiting until later tonight."

"Sure, we can do that," he said, closing his laptop. "It sounds more fun than my month-end accounting, anyway."

I placed my laptop on the table and my phone between us. "So, when we stopped last time, you had just left Santa Rosa."

"I think that's right," he said, taking a sip of his coffee. "Let's see…I remember, once I got my car back, I was just going to make a straight shot of it. I drove twelve or thirteen hours straight with nothing but a pack of Nekot cookies and a liter bottle of Pepsi. I stopped to get gas, of course, but I was determined to make it to L.A. before calling it a day. And when I hit San Bernadino, I thought I was there. But then I realized I was still about sixty or seventy miles from Hollywood. It was late, and I was tired, so I stopped and got a motel room. I remember the Asian woman I woke up in the office sold me a room for twenty dollars."

I had to laugh. "That's four times what you paid in Santa Rosa."

"And it wasn't any nicer," he said. "I had to pay cash up front, and she refused to give me a room key. She fussed at me in her own language all the way to the room. I had no idea what she was saying. After she let me in, I had to prop the door open with a pillow so I could get my stuff in from my car."

Despite my mother's comment about my dad's imagination, the details of his story still left me feeling puzzled. It seemed like he had really been there.

"My audition was at one o'clock the next day," he continued, "so I found my way to the beach in the morning. I mean, I couldn't drive all the way to California and not see the ocean."

"Good call. Which beach did you go to?"

"I didn't really know at the time. I just drove through a canyon from the freeway until I saw the ocean. It turned out to be the north end of Malibu. But it wasn't what I expected."

"Why not?"

"Well, the water was flat and cold and there was no one around. I don't know why, but I was expecting big waves and surfers and whatnot. Maybe I was thinking of Hawaii."

"It was November, wasn't it? You didn't go swimming, did you?"

"Oh, gosh no. I was dressed and ready for my audition. I just put my feet in for a second."

"So, tell me about the big audition."

"Well, it was in this building in Hollywood on Sunset Boulevard. You could drive right by it and not notice it. Nothing really special looking about it. All Gina said was I was supposed to ask for a guy named Troy Lechefsky. So, I found a place to park a few blocks away, grabbed my guitar, and headed up the street."

৩৵৵

As Phillip walked along Sunset Boulevard, any notions he carried of Hollywood being star-filled and glamorous quickly evaporated. After being propositioned by a Camaro-driving man without pants, he quickened his pace past mohawked punk rockers in combat boots, sex shops, pawn shops, and an assortment of sketchy-looking pedestrians. Double-checking the address on Gina's handwritten note, he stopped underneath a blue canvas awning providing shade for an elderly homeless gentleman. Sporting a cowboy hat, he lay resting on the concrete sidewalk gazing up at Phillip.

"How's it going," Phillip said to the man, expecting him to ask for money, food, or alcohol.

"Don't go in there," the old man said.

Amused, Phillip asked, "Why not?"

"They're all in on it."

"In on what?"

"They're coming. The Russians. The police. They're all in on it. Don't go in there."

"Oh, OK. Gotcha," said Phillip, pretending to be serious. "Well, I'll be careful. I promise."

"They're coming. You'll see! They're all in on it!"

Phillip backed slowly away, opened the door of the studio, and stepped inside. Apart from a few poster-sized black and white photos of unnamed musicians on the walls, the lobby was sparsely decorated, and the reception desk sat empty.

"Hello?" Phillip called out modestly.

After a moment, a door to the left of the front desk opened slightly. A woman poked her head out and looked at Phillip. "Oh. Sorry," she said, entering the room. "I was afraid you were that old cowboy out there."

"Interesting guy," said Phillip.

She smiled. "What can I do for you?"

"I'm here to see Troy Lechefsky. I have an audition."

"You're Phillip Johnson."

"Yes."

"Come right this way."

Phillip followed the woman down a long hallway past several closed doors with recording indicators lit above them.

Stopping at the end of the hallway, she turned the corner and pointed. "Go down this way; your live room is the third door on your right. Just go on in and get comfortable. You can warm up if you need to. Mr. Lechefsky will be with you shortly."

∽∾

"So, did you know what you were going to sing for them or how does that work?" I asked.

"Gina had given me two songs to perform. I didn't like one of them, so I substituted a Bob Seger song that I liked. But the one she was really hot about was by John Cougar Mellencamp.

It had just come out, and I was still trying to learn it. But she thought it was perfect for me. When I got in the room, it was completely empty, except for a C12 microphone on a stand."

"I'm sorry, I don't know microphones; what is that?"

"Oh, the C12 is one of those long, tube microphones. It's about a foot long; you've seen them. They're mostly for voice and acoustic pieces."

"Got it; so how did it go?"

∞∞

Phillip opened the door of the studio cautiously, unsure what or who he would find. Other than a single microphone perched on a stand, the small, square, white-painted room was completely vacant. Behind a glass panel on the front wall, the control room was dark and empty. Phillip removed his guitar from its case and slipped the strap over his shoulder. He took a moment to tune each string before playing scales to warm his fingers. After a few minutes, the lights came on in the control room. Phillip could see two middle-aged men taking their places behind the control panel. From the speaker above his head, Phillip heard, "Good afternoon, Phillip. I'm Troy Lechefsky."

"Hey, Mr. Lechefsky. Thanks for having me here."

"Our pleasure. How do you know Mr. Hazelton?"

"I date his daughter."

"Has he heard you perform?"

"Um, no, not really. His daughter Gina, my girlfriend, manages my band, so..."

"I see. Girlfriend and manager. OK. Well, whenever you're ready Phillip. By the way, is that the name you go by on stage? Phillip Johnson?"

"Yes, sir. Why?"

"It's just pretty generic, that's all."

Phillip couldn't argue the point and had nothing to add. "Oh, well...," he said, meekly.

"Anyway, whenever you're ready. Show us what you've got, Phillip."

"OK, I'd like to play a song that's been a favorite—"

"You don't need to do an intro," said Mr. Lechefsky. "Just go ahead."

"Oh, sorry."

His anxiety rising, Phillip started strumming the opening chords of *Shame on the Moon* by Bob Segar. As he worked through the chord progression of G, D, E minor, and C, he began to sing the first verse.

Mr. Lechefsky interrupted, "Can you stand closer to the microphone, Phillip?"

"Sure, sorry."

"OK, start again."

Phillip played the intro chords again and began singing when the other man in the control room interrupted.

"Hey, kid," the man said, "What else do you have?"

"Um," said Phillip, taking a moment to gather himself. "OK, how about this." He started playing the initial G major/C riff of *Pink Houses* by John Cougar Mellencamp and led into the first verse. As he sang, he could see the two men talking to each other behind the glass. It didn't appear they were even listening.

"OK, Phillip," said Mr. Lechefsky over the speaker.

Phillip stopped playing.

"Do you have anything original?" he asked. "Anything you wrote?"

"Um, no," answered Phillip. "I haven't written anything, yet."

"OK, thanks, Phillip."

Phillip paused for a moment, waiting for further direction as he watched the two men talk to each other. "So, do you want me to keep playing?"

"No, we're good," said Mr. Lechefsky. "We'll be in touch with Mr. Hazelton. Thanks for coming out, Phillip."

ও৵

After listening to my dad recount his audition experience, I asked, "You drove all the way across the country for that?"

"Yep. It took less than five minutes. Then I drove back home."

"Wow. So, what happened after that? What did you tell Gina?"

My father took a sip from his coffee. "Why don't we save that for next time," he said, reaching for his laptop. "I should probably get back to my accounting. Reality beckons."

THIRTEEN

The Big Question

When I got home from the café after working with my dad, I realized I had once again failed to discuss the issue of him seeing a doctor despite my renewed promise to my mother. However, he seemed fine the entire time I was with him. No lost personal items or forgotten names. Just regular old time traveler Dad. Regardless, I did commit myself to having that discussion again the next time we met, which raised another issue in my mind. Perhaps the practice of binge-watching streaming TV shows with Elizabeth had shortened my attention span for plot development, but I was growing impatient with the downtime between our weekly story sessions. I freely admit that I may have been masking my impatience with Elizabeth, but I asked my dad if we could meet more than once a week. He replied to my text with a smiley-face emoji. I assumed that meant yes. We planned to meet again Friday around 11:00.

Thursday morning, after a long night staring at the ceiling wondering what the rest of my life would look like without Elizabeth, I finally decided to send her a text message. Nothing serious or imposing. Just a verbal ping to let her know I was still around. "Hey, just checking on you," I typed. She replied quickly.

> Well, hello. I was beginning to think
> I would never hear from you again.

> Um, you were the one who wanted
> a break, not me. I was just doing what
> you wanted.

She didn't respond immediately. Reading it again, I realized how testy my message sounded. After waiting a long thirty seconds, I could see she was typing a response. I prepared myself for the worst.

> This obviously isn't working, Daniel.

> You mean us?

> No. This. The break. Can we have
> lunch or something? To talk?

> Sure. Anytime.

> I'm off tomorrow. How about Groucho's
> at 11:30?

> See you there.

Realizing I had just double-booked myself for Friday, I rescheduled with my dad for Saturday morning at his house and spent the next twenty-six hours in relationship purgatory. But eleven-thirty Friday finally arrived, and I watched Elizabeth make her way into Groucho's Deli right on time.

Groucho's had been in business in Columbia's Five Points shopping district since the 1940s. And though I didn't know Elizabeth in college, we were both regulars there during our time in school. Once we started dating, it naturally became our default choice for a quick, casual lunch together.

She saw me at our usual booth but didn't wave or make eye contact as she approached. Taking a seat across from me, she simply said, "Hi."

"Hi," I replied. After an awkward pause, I added, "So, how are you?"

Seeming distracted and a bit nervous, she asked, "Can we order first?"

"Sure," I said, glancing around for help.

We both ordered the same turkey sandwich every time we ate at Groucho's, hers without bacon. As soon as our favorite server, Kayla, saw us she stopped by our table, confirmed our order, and left.

"So, let me try again," I said, "how are you?"

She cast her eyes out the window next to us. "Daniel, I need to confess something."

"Uh-oh. That doesn't sound good."

"It's about us taking a break," she said, looking back at me. "And I hope you're not going to get mad at me."

"That all depends," I said, only half-joking.

"Just promise."

"OK, I promise I won't get mad at you."

"Or your mother," she added, breaking eye contact.

"My mother? What does she have to do with…" I stopped and let the wheels turn in my head. Everything started to click. "Wait a minute," I said, "you mean…"

She knew where my mind was going. "Uh-huh," she said sheepishly.

"This whole needing a break thing was my mother's idea?"

"Not entirely," she said, "but mostly. She thought it might motivate you."

"Motivate me? To do what?"

"Hello? Think about it. Me? You?"

I made the connection. "To propose, you mean?"

"Yay, you got it," she cheered dryly.

"But how was breaking up with me supposed to make me propose to you?"

"You know, the whole 'absence makes the heart grow fonder' thing. But I didn't know you'd ghost me."

"Ghost you? You said you needed some space. So, I gave it to you."

"For almost three weeks? You don't call or text me for three weeks?"

"Liz, you did this. Or my mother did. So don't get mad at me about it. Besides, why didn't you just ask me how I felt about things?"

"Because you're the one who's supposed to be pursuing *me*. I felt like you were taking me for granted or something."

Kayla arrived with our drinks and sandwiches, placing them on the table before us. And then something really strange happened. I watched Elizabeth glance up, smile, and say thank you. As soon as her blue eyes returned to mine, a chill ran through my entire body. Suddenly, I knew. I was ready to spend the rest of my life with her. "So," I said, going with that impulse, "this whole thing was about getting me to propose, huh?"

"I'm sorry. I'm so embarrassed. But yes."

I gave her a sly smile. "You just said yes."

"Very funny. But you're not getting off that easy."

"OK, fine. How about this, then: Elizabeth, will you marry me?"

She looked horrified. "You did *not* just do that."

My smile disappeared. "Do what?" I asked, unsure what was happening.

"Propose to me at Groucho's over a turkey sandwich."

The best I could get out was, "Um…"

She looked down at her lunch and added, "And they forgot to leave the bacon off. Dang it." Her focus back on me, she added, "So, that's it, then? No ring? No romance? Why not just buy me a juicer, Daniel?"

Trying to recompose myself, I said, "Now, come on, don't be like that. I was serious."

"I know you were. That's the problem." She looked out the window again and shook her head. I had never seen her so upset.

"OK, look, let me try again," I offered. "Tonight. I'll come over. I'll have a ring and everything."

"No, it's done. This is one question you don't get to do over again."

"Why?"

"Because it's already out there," she said, waving her hands.

We sat quietly for a moment. She glared at the bacon on her sandwich while I searched for something to say. "Well, what do we do, then?" I finally asked.

Elizabeth sighed. "Whatever. Fine, I'll marry you."

"So…is that a yes?" I asked hopefully.

She shrugged without looking at me and said, "Sure, why not."

I needed a little more confirmation than that. "You're sure."

"Yes, I'm sure," she said impatiently as she looked back out the window.

"Because you seem kind of down about it."

Her head spun back to me. "Daniel, you don't understand. This is supposed to be one of those moments a girl dreams about. And I promise you, it doesn't happen over lunch at Groucho's."

I couldn't think of a quick, comforting response to that. But as she picked the bacon bits off the top of her sandwich with mild irritation, I finally said, "I love you, you know."

She dropped her shoulders, looked at me, and said, "I know. But you have some serious making up to do."

Then I asked the really big question. "Do you want to call my mom, or should I?"

FOURTEEN

Give Me A Reason

Elizabeth decided we should wait to deliver the news about our engagement. While I had suggested we drive out to my parents' house immediately after our lunch at Groucho's, she wanted a ring on her finger before she told anyone. I suspected she also wanted time to invent a better proposal story than the thoughtless one I had given her. So, when I arrived at my parents' house that Saturday morning, our big news remained a secret.

My mother had made plans to go shopping with some friends and wasn't home, but I did keep the promise I made to her. "Dad, before we get started," I said as we settled at the kitchen table, "I need to talk with you again about something, and you're not going to like it."

"If this is about me going to see a doctor, there's no need."

"Dad, you've got to realize—"

"I've already made an appointment," he said interrupting me.

"What? Really? How did that happen?"

"Well, I've just struggled with some stupid little things lately in front of your mother. And I could see how much she was stressing about it. So, I did it for her. I have an appointment next month."

"Wow, that's a relief, Dad. We just want to be sure you're OK."

"I know, Son. I'm sorry you had to get in the middle of all that. But don't worry. I'm fine."

Thankful to have that burden lifted, I said, "Well, all right then, what do you say we jump back into your story?"

"Are you recording?"

I pressed the button on my phone. "OK, we're rolling. So, what happened when you got back to Columbia after your audition?"

"Let's see…it took me the better part of three days to get back across the country. And by the time I got home to my apartment and called Gina, she had already heard from her dad."

"I'm guessing she wasn't happy."

"No, she wasn't. She broke up with me."

"Wow. Over the phone?"

"Yep. And she told me she was kicking me out of the band, too."

"What a…," I said, censoring myself.

My dad chuckled. "Yes, she was," he said. "But my time with the band wasn't quite over. I still had one last gig to play the next night at Greene Streets. And that's when I finally met Vallie."

❧

The Friday after Phillip's return from his unsuccessful label audition, the Sole Winners took the stage before a capacity crowd at Greene Streets. Phillip did his best to mimic the vocals of popular songs like *Every Breath You Take* by the Police, *Cuts Like a Knife* by Bryan Adams, and *Separate Ways* by Journey. But having just been rejected in Hollywood for attempting to do the same thing, his heart wasn't in it. Not that it mattered. He knew cold beer and loud music were enough to satisfy the Columbia bar crowd.

Halfway through their first set, in between songs, Phillip's attention was drawn to the edge of the stage. An attractive college-age brunette was waving him over. Kneeling down to her, he asked, "Something you'd like to hear?"

"I want you to sing a song to my friend," she said. "I'm trying to keep her from driving to Charleston to see her boyfriend tonight."

"What's your friend's name?"

"It's Vallie."

"Anything in particular?" asked Phillip, not realizing Vallie was, in fact, Valerie Ray.

"Do you know any country songs?" she asked. "She likes that stuff."

"How about something by George Strait?" suggested Phillip.

"I don't know who that is, but sure. And make sure you look at her when you sing. Sing it to her." She held up a ten-dollar bill. "And I'll give you ten bucks if you come talk to her."

Phillip took the bill and stuffed it in his pocket. "Where is she?"

"We're over there," she said, pointing up and to her left.

Phillip's eyes followed the direction of her arm and saw Valerie Ray standing behind the second-tier railing. "That's Valerie," he said, not believing his luck.

"You know her?" the girl asked.

"No, but she came in where I work once."

"Wait, I remember you. You're the check-cashing guy at the drugstore."

Michael called out impatiently from behind his drums, "Phillip!"

"OK, OK," Phillip said to Michael with a dismissive wave. Turning back to the girl, he smiled and gave her an affirming nod as he stood to his feet. Stepping over to the microphone, he found Vallie again in the crowd and said, "Our next song is a special request. This one's for you, Vallie. I hope you stay a while."

Phillip turned around to face his band. "This is a country song, guys. It's called *A Fire I Can't Put Out*. It's in the key of D. Just follow my lead."

"Gina said no country songs," said Michael, pointing a drumstick at Phillip.

"Fine, Michael, you just sit there and look like an idiot while I play it by myself." Phillip turned and put a capo on his guitar's first fret as he stepped toward the microphone. His electric guitarist stepped over and gently pulled Phillip back a few steps.

"I know the song," said Zack. "I'll cover the violin melody on guitar." Zack turned to face the drums. "Michael, it's a slow one, so go lento on the tempo. Around 51 or 52. Got it?"

Michael nodded and gave a complicit shrug of his shoulders.

Phillip watched Zack and their bass player, Braden, exchange confirming looks. Facing his bandmates, Phillip counted up to the first beat, then began strumming his guitar as he turned to the microphone. Zack joined in right on cue and plucked a pleasant country twang on his electric guitar. Phillip strummed along as Michael and Braden added a light beat.

Whenever Phillip played this George Strait song alone in his apartment, he would close his eyes and picture Valerie in his mind. And now with eyes wide open, he sang it to the same beautiful face.

When the song was over and the applause faded, Phillip let the crowd know the band would be taking a short break. He lifted the strap off his shoulder and placed his guitar on its stand.

"Phillip, what are you doing?" asked Michael. "We don't take a break until the end of this set."

"Fine, keep playing without me; I don't care," said Phillip as he walked toward the stairs leading off the stage. Once on the floor, he made his way up the side stairs to the second tier and found Vallie smiling as he approached.

Her friend offered an introduction. "Vallie, this is…"

"Phillip," he said not taking his eyes off Vallie. "It's nice to meet you, Vallie."

Her friend added, "He remembered you from when you came in his store a few months ago."

"Where was that?" asked Vallie.

"At the drugstore on Sumter Street," said Phillip.

"You cashed my check!" Vallie said.

"You remember," said Phillip, pleased.

"I thought you looked familiar up there. And thanks for the song, by the way. I love George Strait."

"He's one of my favorites," said Phillip. Vallie's friend gave him a gentle bump with her elbow. Taking the hint, Phillip said, "So, I hear you might head to Charleston tonight."

"I might," said Vallie, with a shrug.

Phillip glanced at her friend before adding, "We were – I mean, I – was kind of hoping you'd hang around."

A playful grin appeared on Vallie's face. "Give me a reason," she said.

"OK, well…," Phillip began, unsure what that reason might be. But he felt sure Vallie was flirting with him, so he decided to go for broke. "How about we head to my place, and I can play some more country songs for you. And then we can listen to George Strait all night."

"You mean after your show? That's kind of late."

"How 'bout right now, then?" asked Phillip, impulsively.

"What about your band?" she asked. "Aren't you supposed to get back up there?"

"Oh, they're fine without me. What do you say?"

Vallie studied Phillip for a moment. "You'd really do that for me?"

"Sure," said Phillip, seeing an opportunity to flirt back. "Just give me a reason."

Vallie looked at Phillip and flashed the same smile he remembered from the drugstore.

"That's good enough for me," he said.

§

"So, did you two go hang out at your place?" I asked.

"We did. I grabbed my guitar off the stage, told the guys they were on their own, and left with Vallie. We did exactly what I said we'd do. We sat on the floor of my den 'til three in the morning."

"Three?"

"Yep. We talked about everything you could think of. I told her about my failed audition in L.A. and about Gina. She told me about her boyfriend in Charleston and how she wasn't sure about him. You want to see what she looked like?"

"Vallie? You have a picture?"

"Kind of," he said. "Hang on a second."

My dad went down the long hallway toward the back of their house. I could hear him going upstairs to his study. After a few minutes, he returned with a piece of paper and told me how he had drawn Vallie's picture that night in his apartment.

§

While Phillip carefully sketched Vallie's face with a pencil sometime after midnight, he listened to her talk about her family in Manning. She joked about her twin sisters' penchant for being insufferable and how small-town life no longer appealed to her. She shared her thoughts on love and her concern for her roommate's disapproval of her boyfriend in Charleston.

Despite Vallie's lively expressions, in his drawing Phillip tried to recreate a subtle glance she had given him earlier in the evening. A glance that told him she might truly be interested.

My father then handed me this:

"You drew this?" I said in amazement.

"I did," he said. "That's not the original one I did for her, but it's a close approximation."

I placed the aged paper carefully on the table as I studied the face before me. "She's beautiful, Dad."

"She definitely was," he said, taking it into his hands. "I'd better put this away before your mom gets home."

When he returned from his study and settled back at the kitchen table, I tried to summarize what I'd been hearing. "It sounds like you and Vallie covered everything there was to do and talk about, all in one night."

"It didn't stop there," he said. "After I finished the drawing, we wrote a song together."

"You wrote a song together?"

"We did. It must have been almost two in the morning when we finished it. It's called *Give Me a Reason*."

"The song you sang for me here a few weeks ago? You wrote that with Vallie?"

He nodded. "We started writing it as a joke, poking fun at how we flirted with each other at Greene Streets. But by the time we finished, we'd written a real country song. It was something else."

৵৽

While Vallie scribbled the words to their collaboration on notebook paper, Phillip toyed with different melodies to match their cadence and mood. After an hour of playful arguments over word choices, song meaning, and perspective, Phillip asked Vallie to hold up their finished lyrics so he could read them while he played the tune on his guitar.

When I hold you in my arms at night
I can feel your heart in tune with mine
And every song
Rings true
There're a lot of words that I'd love to say
They're running through my mind
But they can't find
Their way to you

You know I'd stay
With you tonight

But I just don't know

Cause I'd be anything you want me to be
Your hero, your friend, your meant to be
I'd love you more in every season
I'd tell her goodbye
Just give me a reason

There's a song I've written, I just can't sing
I've tried a thousand times, but still it seems
She's there at home
Waiting for me
If I only knew what's on your mind
Am I in your heart? Or should I leave
This all behind?
I just don't know

You know I'd stay
With you this way
But I have to know

Cause I'd be anything you want me to be
Your hero, your friend, your meant to be
You know I'd love you more in every season
I'd tell her goodbye
Just give me a reason
Please give me a reason

With the last chord still reverberating around the empty room, Vallie rose to her knees, leaned over Phillip's guitar, and kissed him for the first time. "That's our song," she said, her eyes still just inches from his.

Phillip sat speechless, his large smile speaking for him.

"This is mind-blowing," I said.

My dad smiled warmly. "It was the best time I'd ever had with anyone my whole life up to that point." He paused as his smile began to fade. "But…"

"Uh-oh," I said. "I guess I should've expected that."

"Yeah. It was all for nothing."

❧

"What if you had played *that* at your audition?" Vallie posed emphatically. "You'd be a star in no time!"

Still humbled by his record label rejection, Phillip replied, "I don't know about that."

"It's a shame you can't go back and do it over again. You'd blow them away!"

Vallie couldn't have known the seeds she was planting in Phillip's mind. But after he drove her home shortly after three in the morning and kissed her goodnight, her words began repeating in his head and later in his dreams. By early Sunday morning, he was back on the road to Santa Rosa.

❧

The door from the garage suddenly opened into the kitchen. "Hello!" my mom said as she entered the house.

"Shoot," I said, quietly. "I guess we're done for today."

"Looks like it."

"Hey, Mom."

She set a few bags on the kitchen counter and said, "I heard you had lunch with a special someone yesterday."

The grin she was wearing made me uncomfortable. "Um, yeah."

"I think that's wonderful," she said.

"It was," I said, unsure how much she knew.

"Well?" she asked, her hands on her hips.

"Well, what?" I asked innocently.

"Any news for me?"

I played it safe and dumb. "News? Nope. No news."

She furrowed her eyebrows at me. "Well, I'm just glad you two are spending time together again. That Elizabeth is such a sweet girl. It'd be a shame to let her get away."

"Yeah," I said, plainly. When she turned her attention to my dad for a moment, I grabbed my phone and sent Elizabeth a text asking if she had told my mother about my Groucho's proposal. Her quick response was, "No!! And don't you either!" I breathed a sigh of relief.

FIFTEEN

Due West

S ince I had failed to meet Elizabeth's proposal expectations, which by the way were still not clear to me, I decided to ask for her assistance in picking out her engagement ring. Disappointing her twice was a risk I couldn't afford to take. We spent the better part of her next day off visiting every jewelry store in Columbia without deciding on a ring. However, I began to get the feeling that some of my "making up to do" would be in the form of a larger diamond.

Just a few days after my previous story session with my dad, we met again in his café. And I have to admit, I'd been looking forward to continuing the tale, real or not. We sat in the soft leather lounge chairs behind the round coffee table and, after Julia brought his coffee and my water, we got started.

"So, you left me hanging last week," I said.

"That was your mom's doing," he said, sipping his coffee. "She's not letting up on the Elizabeth thing, is she?"

"No, but that's OK," I said. "It'll all work out, I think."

"I hope so."

"So, you said your time with Vallie was wasted or something like that. What happened?"

"OK, well, Vallie's comment about getting a do-over with the record label got me thinking about what Gouyen, the Apache woman, told me about Black Hole. And I wondered, what if it were true? What if you really could go back in time? I was young, stupid, and had no idea how that would work. But since I had absolutely nothing to lose, or so I thought, I decided to go see for myself."

"You drove all the way back out there?"

"I did. I called Vallie from a pay phone when I stopped for gas in Knoxville and left a message with her roommate, the same girl she was with at Greene Streets. I said I was going back to L.A. to try again. Vallie must have told her about our song because she asked if I was going to sing it and wished me luck."

"I have to ask, how many times did you turn around on your way out there?"

My father laughed. "Twice," he admitted. "I did have a few doubts about what I was doing."

"I can imagine. Did you find the two ladies again?"

"I really just needed to find Gouyen, and I did. But I had to fend off a nosey, insightful bartender for a while before I could talk with her."

❧

The drive from South Carolina to New Mexico was slowed by Phillip's second thoughts about the trip. Arguing with himself over the veracity of the Apache woman's time travel claims — combined with his desire to be with Vallie — led him to briefly reverse course on I-40, twice. The first time in Memphis and again in Norman, Oklahoma. But after reaching a point of firm resolution, Phillip continued west, reaching Santa Rosa shortly after two o'clock Tuesday afternoon, tired and slightly irritable.

Leaving his car in the truck stop parking lot, Phillip trotted across the street to the bar, pulled the screened door open, and stepped inside. Except for an elderly couple seated at a table along the far wall, the bartender watched over an empty room.

"He's back," said the bartender as Phillip approached. "Did your car break down again?"

"No," Phillip said, anxious to get to the point. "I was hoping to find Gouyen."

"What for?" he asked.

"Nothing," Phillip said, unwilling to explain.

"Nothing, huh?" said the bartender skeptically. "Look kid, Gouyen's a friend of mine. But if I were you, I wouldn't get too close, if you know what I mean."

Phillip didn't know or care what he meant, so he ignored the warning. "Do you know where I can find her?"

"She's probably working. Down the street at Diane's, the hair place."

"Thanks," said Phillip, turning to leave.

"Hey kid, what's your name again?"

"It's Phillip."

"Just be careful, Phillip."

Unsure what to make of the bartender's concern, Phillip followed the sidewalk a short way down the street to a cream-colored stucco building with a barber pole hanging next to the front door. Pulling the glass door open, he found Gouyen standing in the middle of the room with a broom in her hand, talking with two other women. The customer chairs were empty. Watching Phillip enter and wave hello, Gouyen appeared slightly alarmed.

"Hey, Gouyen," said Phillip. "Can I talk with you for a minute?"

"I'm busy right now," she said, beginning to sweep.

"It's about Black Hole," said Phillip.

Gouyen laughed awkwardly as her eyes bounced quickly between her coworkers. Leaning the broom against a chair, she grabbed Phillip by his arm and hurried him out the door. Once outside, she released him and asked, "What are you doing coming here? Are you trying to get me in trouble?"

Gouyen's aggressive demeanor surprised Phillip. "No," he said defensively, "the bartender told me I could find you here. I want to try the Black Hole and thought you could help me."

After studying Phillip's face for a moment, she seemed to calm down. She glanced back through the glass door at her co-workers and said, "We can't talk here. I get off at three. Meet me at the bar then. But don't tell anyone what you're doing here, especially Elan."

"Who's Elan?"

"The bartender."

"Yeah, he kind of told me to stay away from you. Why would he do that?"

"Don't worry about Elan. He thinks he's looking out for you. Just ignore what he says and give him a nice tip."

Gouyen turned and reentered the barbershop, leaving Phillip alone on the street. He considered hanging out at the truck stop until three o'clock as an alternative to the bar, but the lure of a cold beer led him back to a barstool facing Elan.

"Did you find Gouyen?" Elan asked, placing a cold bottle of Budweiser in front of Phillip.

"Yeah," said Phillip, nodding a thank you to Elan. "I just wanted to say hey, you know. She was nice to me when I came through here last week."

"She showed you around town, right?"

Phillip took a long swig from the bottle. "We went to Blue Hole, yeah," he said.

"Is that it?" asked Elan.

"Yep, that was it," lied Phillip.

"Nowhere else?"

"There's not much else to see, is there?" joked Phillip.

"You've got me there. So, what brings you back today?"

"Oh, I'm just passing through."

"From where to where?"

Elan's relentless interview was becoming annoying. Rather than explaining his travels back and forth across the country, Phillip just said, "I had an audition in Los Angeles with a record label."

"Wow, that's cool. How did it go? Did they sign you?"

Phillip finally had a question he could answer honestly. "No. I don't think I did much to impress them."

"I'm sorry to hear that. What went wrong, do you think?"

"Well for starters, I didn't have any original music. I was just trying to play covers, and they didn't want to hear that. They didn't like my name, either."

"Your name?"

"Phillip Johnson. They said it sounded too generic. The whole thing lasted less than five minutes."

"So, you're headed back home, now?"

Phillip paused as he considered another lie but decided on a partial truth. "Actually, I'm going back out there to try again," he said. "I've written a song of my own, and I think they might like it."

Elan took the towel off his shoulder, picked up a pint glass, and began wiping it, his attention seemingly off Phillip for a moment. Without looking up, he asked, "Is this why you want to see Gouyen?"

"Um...," Phillip said, feeling exposed.

"I thought so," Elan said. "Look kid, I don't mean to get in your business; I'm just trying to be a friend. But can I give you some advice?"

"OK," said Phillip. He was ready to listen.

"First, I'm not going to get into what Gouyen believes or what she's been telling you. That's for her to own and for you to believe or not believe. But just remember this: We're only given one life to live. What we do with that is up to us. Sometimes things don't work out the way we'd like. Sometimes they do. That's life. But when you play with the spirit world and higher powers, you're playing with fire. And people might get hurt, including you."

The creaking sound of the bar's screened door turned Phillip's head as Gouyen appeared in the doorway. "Phillip, come with me," she said, waving him over.

Phillip looked at Elan as he slid off his barstool to join Gouyen.

"Think about it, Phillip," said Elan.

Phillip said nothing as he considered the bartender's advice. He simply gave Elan a slight smile as he turned to leave with Gouyen.

❧

"The bartender sounded like a nice guy," I said.

"He was. But what he didn't realize," my dad explained, "was that his warning only made me believe Gouyen more. I mean, if she was just blowing smoke about Black Hole, he'd have no reason to be concerned, right? So, I thought she must be telling the truth."

"But it sounded like no one believed her," I said, "even her own sister, what's her name."

"Or maybe they knew what she was saying was true but didn't think she should be telling people about it."

"Maybe. But obviously, you decided to trust Gouyen."

"I guess I just wanted to believe it, so yeah. I trusted her."

❧

Phillip followed Gouyen quietly to her car behind the barbershop. They both climbed in, but Gouyen sat behind the wheel with the keys in her hand. "Your sadness has left you, I see," she said.

Equating sadness with Gina, Phillip said, "Um, I guess you could say that."

"Then why did you come back?"

"There's just something I need to do over again," Phillip said.

"I see. And if you do this thing again differently, what do you think will change?"

"Everything," Phillip said, confidently. "My whole life will change."

Gouyen nodded approvingly. "As long as you understand."

"Will you show me?"

"I already have shown you," she said. "This is something you must do alone."

"So, what then? I just go into the cave? Is that it?"

"As I told you before, enter Black Hole before the sun rises. Walk a straight path into the darkness. And emerge with the rising sun to a younger day."

"But how does it know where, I mean what day I want to go to?"

"If you don't trust the Spirit that leads you, there is no reason to follow. The choice is yours. But if you do, just remember, walk a straight path." Gouyen put her key in the ignition and started the car.

"Where are we going?" asked Phillip.

"I'm going home," said Gouyen. "You can get out now."

"OK, well. Thanks," said Phillip as he opened the door. "I'll let you know how it goes."

"No, you won't. Goodbye, Phillip."

∽∾

"So, she left you on your own? I thought she would at least take you out into the desert again."

"No, I had to figure that out myself. From what she said, I was supposed to go into the cave before the sun came up. So that afternoon before it got dark, I found the dirt trail back to the river, so I'd be able to find it in the morning. And I stayed out of the bar to avoid Elan and anyone else who might be in there."

"Did you get your five-dollar motel room again?"

"No, I slept in my car in the truck stop parking lot to save a few bucks."

"You couldn't afford five dollars?"

"Trust me, I was running pretty low on cash."

ஒ⌀⌀

As another large truck rumbled past Phillip's car in the truck stop parking lot, he finally gave up on sleep. He turned the key in the ignition just enough to check the time on his dashboard clock. It was a little after 5:30 AM. He sat up, adjusted the seat back to driving position, and rubbed his hands over his tired face. After a quick trip inside the truck stop to grab a Pepsi and visit the restroom, he felt ready for his visit to Black Hole.

ஒ⌀⌀

As we talked, my dad's eyes kept looking over my shoulder. I finally turned around to see a long line at the cash register.

"Sorry to leave you hanging again, Son," my dad said, "but it looks like we're short-handed tonight. Can we stop there? I need to give Julia and Kelly a hand."

"No worries, Dad. We'll pick it up there, next time."

As my father stepped away, I sent Elizabeth a text message asking if she wanted to go ring shopping on her next day off. Her response left me a little puzzled. "That's OK," it read. "No hurry on that."

SIXTEEN

A Younger Day

Despite the fact that Elizabeth and I were engaged, at least technically, I was beginning to get mixed signals. Since our "break" was over, I assumed she'd want to jump back into our usual nighttime routines of dinner, dog walks, and TV watching. Instead, she responded to my invitations with text messages about how she was tired or not feeling well. I considered just dropping by her house to see her, but the last time I did that she broke up with me. So, I tried to remain patient, hoping she really was just tired or not feeling well. But when my mother asked why Elizabeth wasn't returning her calls or texts, I knew we had a problem.

In short, Elizabeth was taking a real break. Her growing impatience with the long-term status of our relationship, combined with my "ghosting" her for three weeks and my turkey sandwich marriage proposal, were enough. I had unwittingly embodied the persona of a thoughtless, unromantic, non-committal boyfriend who took her for granted. And despite my love for her, I was at a loss for ways to remedy the situation.

With the end of my summer break just a few weeks away, I put even more urgency into scheduling time with my dad. Our sessions also provided a helpful diversion from my Elizabeth problem. The Wednesday following our time in his café, we met at my house. I was anxious to hear him describe his visit to Black Hole. Time travel was the hook of his story, after all, and I was ready to hear the details.

"So, are we there yet?" I asked jokingly as I began recording.

"Almost," said my dad. "But first, I had to find my way to Black Hole in the dark."

ক৵৵

Once Phillip found the horse trail leading to the Pecos River canyon, driving on it in the dark wasn't as difficult as he feared, particularly at just five miles per hour. Though he had considered leaving his car by the road and just walking the path to the river, the occasional glow of unknown animal eyes watching his slow progress made him glad he drove. When he reached the trees lining the top of the canyon just before six AM, Phillip stopped, turned off his car, and placed his keys in his cup holder. He sat motionless for a moment, staring blankly into the dimly lit predawn landscape. "This is so stupid," he said, shaking his head at himself. Nevertheless, a curious hope pushed him out of his car and on toward the river.

Stepping carefully through the trees and bushes while watching and listening for rattlesnakes, Phillip reached the east side of the canyon. Across the river at the base of the hill sat the dark shadow of Black Hole. He climbed over the smooth boulders forming the edge of the sloping canyon wall and descended slowly toward the river bottom. Only a foot or two deep, the slow-moving water made for easy crossing.

Once on the other side, Phillip could see into the mouth of the cave ahead. He stepped forward slowly, the smell of sulfur growing stronger as he neared the entrance. Standing before the large opening, he called out, "Hello!" just for good measure. As the echo faded, he slowly entered the darkness. Gouyen's words, "walk a straight path," repeated in his head with each step until he was unable to see his hand before his face. Without looking back, Phillip passed into the abyss of Black Hole.

჻჻჻

"So, how far into the cave did you go?" I asked.

"Well, that's the thing. All Gouyen told me was just to walk a straight path. I assumed that was to keep me from getting lost in the cave. So, I expected to come out the other side of the hill. And this is where things got fuzzy, but eventually–"

"You mean like after a few minutes?" I asked.

"No, it's hard to say how long it took. It's weird. But at some point, I started to see light from the cave exit. So, I just kept walking toward it. And then I woke up."

"What do you mean you woke up?" I asked.

"I woke up in my five-dollar-a-night motel room, there in Santa Rosa."

"You mean you dreamed the whole thing?"

"That's what I thought, at first. But remember, the night before I went in Black Hole, I slept in my car. I didn't get a motel room."

I saw an opportunity to challenge the logic of my dad's story. "Yeah, but why didn't you just come back out of the cave instead of waking up in the motel?"

"Because when the sun came up that day the first time," he explained, "that's where I was. I was in my motel room bed. When Black Hole sent me back to that day, to be anywhere else would involve moving in time *and* space. Those are two different dimensions."

"You're doing your amateur quantum physicist thing again," I said, feeling a little disadvantaged.

"Anyway," he continued, "sitting there in the bed, I started wondering if something really did happen in Black Hole."

I decided to give my side of the argument one more try. "But maybe this *was* the first time you woke up there, and you just imagined all the rest over time, instead of the other way around."

"Son, that's even more confusing than what I'm trying to tell you."

I shrugged and said, "Just a thought."

"Anyway, I got up and looked out the window and saw my car in the parking lot outside the mechanic's garage, just like the week before."

For my last rebuttal, I said, "Maybe it got towed in from the desert somehow."

My father gave me a quick, patronizing smile and continued. "I sat there on my bed for a while not really sure what to do or what to think. My wallet was on the nightstand, and I noticed it had a lot more cash in it than I had driving out there. Finally, just to clear my head, I took a quick, cold shower."

"Still no hot water?"

"Same as before. I got dressed and decided to walk over to the garage. They had just opened, and the manager was in there talking with the mechanic who'd worked on my car before."

ༀ

When Phillip opened the door of the garage office, he was greeted by the same round, smiling, Hispanic man who arranged for his car to be towed a week ago. "Hola, Señior Johnson," the manager said with a smile. "We got your car towed in late yesterday. It's first in line this morning."

Phillip stood speechless as he watched the manager hand Nitis, the mechanic, his car keys. Nitis breezed by Phillip into the parking lot and, with the help of two other men, pushed his car into an open garage bay.

"So, you haven't fixed the starter yet?" asked Phillip, trying to understand what was happening and when.

"You think it's the starter?" the manager asked.

"That's what Nitis said."

"He hasn't looked at it yet, but it could be. He's out there with it now, so it shouldn't take long. You're welcome to have a seat and wait for it. Here's a newspaper if you'd like something to read."

Phillip took the newspaper and sat down. He noticed the week-old date on the *Albuquerque Journal* and asked, "Do you have today's paper?"

"That *is* today's paper," said the manager.

It was then that Phillip truly accepted the reality of Black Hole. He had emerged with the rising sun to a younger day, just as Gouyen said. And it was the same day he first left Santa Rosa for Los Angeles. "My audition is tomorrow," he said quietly to himself. He didn't understand it, but Phillip would have his second chance.

ॐ

As I listened to my dad's story, I felt similar to the way he described his own reaction. I didn't understand it, but I found myself slowly beginning to wonder if it could be true. At a minimum, I felt conflicted about what I was hearing. My dad took note of my unusual silence.

"No questions for me about that?" he asked.

"Um, not right now," I said. "I'm just trying to take it all in."

He smiled and said, "That's exactly how I felt."

SEVENTEEN

Do Over

While my mother continued to give me updates on my dad's memory issues, Pumpkin's weight, and the odd places she'd found his car keys or reading glasses, I hadn't noticed any mental lapses the last few times I'd been with him. Perhaps the comfort in knowing he had an upcoming doctor's appointment made me less attuned, but I heard nothing of concern when playing back our recordings, either. However, with time travel now fully on the table, the salient question wasn't dementia as much as it was sanity. That feels like an overstatement, particularly since I found myself considering the possibility of truth in my father's story. As a teacher of high school students, I had significant experience discerning truth from lies. And I didn't believe my father was lying. Nor did he seem to be creating fanciful stories just for entertainment value. He had truly experienced something. Something real to him, at least.

When we met again just two days after our last talk, our story moved from Santa Rosa to Los Angeles. We settled in my parents' den, with me on the couch and my father in his recliner. Pumpkin and Bono took naps on the rug at my father's feet.

"So," I began, "you did the same drive again, with Nekots and Pepsi, all the way to San Bernardino?"

"I did. I even woke up the Asian woman in the same motel, just for fun."

"Did you go to the beach again?"

"No. Since I'd already seen it, I practiced *Give Me a Reason* in my room until the woman kicked me out at eleven o'clock. I couldn't find the paper with the lyrics in my car, so I just had to go by memory. But I thought it sounded pretty good. I was excited about the audition."

"So, no John Cougar Mellencamp this time?"

He laughed. "No. This time was going to be different. I still had the image issue, though."

"What issue?"

"The Phillip Johnson issue. My name was boring."

"No more boring than George Jones," I offered.

"That was a different time when he came along. I needed a name that just said *country music* when you heard it."

I tried to think of a good country pun. "How about Billy Hill? Get it? Hillbilly…Billy Hill?"

"Subtle," my dad said with a grin.

Then I remembered. "Wait, you said you went by Walker Owens, right?"

My father smiled and nodded.

ꝏᴥ

On the drive to the studio in Hollywood, Phillip gave thought to a stage name he might claim as his own, preferably something with a country flair. But nothing original came to mind. George was already taken. Hank was too obvious. When he neared the studio on Sunset Boulevard, all he had was Phillip Johnson. He parked in the same spot as before but walked on the opposite side of the street to avoid being solicited by the pantless man in the Camaro. Crossing the street to the awning-covered studio entrance, Phillip noticed the same homeless man as before resting on the sidewalk.

"Don't go in there," the man said, right on cue.

"I know," said Phillip, "they're all in on it."

"They are!" the man said, sitting up straight.

Phillip whispered, "And the Russians, too."

The man's eyes grew wider. "And the police!" he said.

"Oh, yeah," said Phillip. "Can't forget about them." Suddenly, Phillip took note of the man's weathered cowboy hat. "Say, I'll give you five dollars for that hat."

Without hesitation, the man removed the hat from his head and held it up to Phillip. "Just don't tell them where you got it," he said.

"It'll be our secret," said Phillip, taking a five-dollar bill from his wallet and handing it to the man. As Phillip placed the hat on his head and turned to walk inside, he stopped and asked, "What's your name, old-timer?"

"Walker Owens," the man said, examining the five-dollar bill.

Phillip smiled. "That's perfect."

∽∾

"Didn't the studio people recognize the hat from the homeless guy?" I asked my dad.

"The receptionist did when she came out, but I explained and asked her not to tell anyone. She said Mr. Lechefsky never came in or out the front door, anyway, so he wouldn't know."

∽∾

Phillip entered the empty recording studio just as before, removed his guitar from its case, checked the tuning, and stepped up to the microphone. While he waited for the lights to come on behind the glass, he casually strummed the chords from his song, visualizing Vallie sitting before him in his apartment. The memory calmed his nerves as he smiled to himself.

137

When the lights came on in the control room, Phillip watched Mr. Lechefsky and the same man as before take their seats. From the ceiling speaker, he heard the familiar greeting.

"Good afternoon, Phillip. I'm Troy Lechefsky."

"Hey, Mr. Lechefsky. Thanks for having me here."

"Our pleasure. How do you know Mr. Hazelton?"

"I used to date his daughter."

"Has he heard you perform?"

"No, sir."

"I see. Well, whenever you're ready Phillip. By the way, is that the name you go by on stage? Phillip Johnson?"

"No, actually I go by Walker Owens."

"Nice. And the hat, is that part of the look?"

"Yes, sir. I'm going to play a country song I wrote, so the hat kind of goes with it."

"Well, you're in luck, Phillip. The gentleman to my right is David Stanley from our Nashville subsidiary. He's visiting us today and is always looking for country music talent."

Mr. Stanley asked, "And this is a song you wrote, yourself, son?"

"Yes, sir. It's called *Give Me a Reason*."

"OK, whenever you're ready, Phillip," said Mr. Lechefsky. "Show us what you've got."

Phillip stepped closer to the microphone and began playing. His modest goal, given his previous experience, was just to get through the first verse without being stopped by Mr. Lechefsky. But when he reached the second verse uninterrupted, he began to relax and enjoy the feel of the song as he performed. When he had finished, he opened his eyes and waited for comment from the two men.

"Just one sec, Phillip," said Mr. Lechefsky.

Phillip waited anxiously as he watched the two men talk behind the glass, unsure what would happen next.

Mr. Stanley spoke first. "Phillip, we really enjoyed that. Have you written anything else?"

"I'm working on a few things," Phillip fibbed. "But nothing I can play right now." Phillip waited while the two men talked.

Mr. Stanley seemed rather enthusiastic as he talked with Mr. Lechefsky. He turned his attention back to Phillip and said, "Phillip, you're from South Carolina, is that correct?"

"Yes, sir."

"How did you get out here?" Mr. Stanley asked.

"I drove."

Their mic was off, but Phillip could see the men laughing as they continued their conversation.

Finally, Mr. Lechefsky said, "Phillip would you join us in the control room? Just go out the way you came in, then it's the first door on your left."

❧

"Did they sign you?" I asked.

"Well, first, they asked if I had an agent. And like an idiot, the only name I could think of was Gina. They asked if I had signed anything with her, and I was able to say no. That seemed to speed things up a bit. Mr. Lechefsky said he'd contact Mr. Hazelton and take care of everything else. I didn't have any idea what he meant, but that afternoon, I was on a private plane with Mr. Stanley to Nashville."

"What about your car?"

"They said not to worry about it. They'd have it sent to me. Besides, Mr. Stanley said he was sure I'd be driving a new one soon. They wanted to get me in the studio and cut a record as soon as possible. I couldn't wait to tell Vallie."

EIGHTEEN

Oversight

My mother got home just after my dad finished describing his label audition do-over. He left me with a host of questions, but they would have to wait. My mother wanted to talk about Elizabeth, of course. Though I tried to reassure her that we would work things out, it seemed we both shared a lack of confidence in my ability to make that happen. Regardless, I begged her to stay out of it. And though I made her promise to stop contacting Elizabeth, my girlfriend history said that was highly unlikely.

When my dad and I met again two days later, we were back in his coffee shop. People were sitting in our usual soft leather chairs, and, despite my encouragement, my dad refused to use owner privilege to make them move. So, we sat on bar stools at the large community table. Fortunately, it was just the two of us.

"So, Dad, let's talk about time travel stuff," I said, opening my laptop and beginning to record.

"OK. What do you want to know?"

"Well, I know you've studied all the quantum mechanics and physics theories and stuff like that."

"I wouldn't say I've studied," he said, "Let's just say I've read a lot on the subject. Something I wish I'd done before I actually did it."

"Why do you say that?"

"Because, when I decided to go back out to Santa Rosa to visit Black Hole, I was only focused on one thing: getting another chance at my audition. I was happy to be free from Gina, and I had just met Vallie. And I thought if I could only get a second chance in L.A., everything would be perfect. I never gave a thought to how that may affect anything else."

"That's what I had a question about. Did anything change after you went back?"

"That's putting it mildly."

∾

Following his audition, Phillip moved his car to the label's gated parking lot behind the studio as Mr. Lechefsky had instructed. He removed his overnight bag and left the car key with his secretary. While at her desk, Phillip asked to use a phone to make a long-distance call. The secretary led him to a large conference room and showed him how to use the phone on the table. Once alone, Phillip dialed Vallie's dormitory phone number and listened to it ring. Her roommate answered.

"May I speak to Vallie?" he asked, trying to contain his enthusiasm.

"Who may I say is calling?"

"It's Phillip."

"Vallie, it's some guy named Phillip. He sounds excited about something."

After a moment, he heard Vallie's voice. "Hello?" she said.

"Vallie, I did it! I sang our song, and they loved it!"

"Who is this?"

"It's me, Phillip."

"I don't know a Phillip."

"Phillip! We hung out at my place Friday night."

"Um, I was in Charleston with my boyfriend last weekend."

"No, I—"

"Sorry, you've got the wrong number. Goodbye."

Phillip heard the call end with a click. His mind raced for an explanation as he slowly lowered the phone onto its base. Taking a seat at the table, his eyes widened and his heart sank as a new reality began to reveal itself.

❦

"Vallie didn't know who you were?" I asked.

"She couldn't. Remember, I met her a few days after my first audition. That was in the past for me, but still in the future for her."

"But you wrote the song together," I said, "the one you sang at the audition."

"We did. But she hadn't yet."

I shook my head. "This stuff will give you a headache."

"It gets worse," he said. "I was still with Gina."

❦

Gina received a call from her father two hours after Phillip's audition. While initially unhappy to hear of his rogue country performance, her mood softened as her father explained that Phillip had walked into a perfect, if not coincidental, opportunity.

David Stanley had flown to Los Angeles to meet with Troy Lechefsky about sourcing new country music talent for their label in Nashville. Mr. Stanley's top writers had supplied enough songs to fill an album; all he needed was a new artist to record them. Their discussion over lunch carried into Phillip's scheduled audition time, which Mr. Lechefsky assured would only be a five-minute interruption at most. After all, the

143

audition was simply an obligatory favor. But when Phillip stepped up to the microphone, he played right into Mr. Stanley's plans.

Gina's father also informed Mr. Stanley that she would be Phillip's manager. Within hours after the call with her father, she was on a plane to Nashville. And when Phillip watched Gina bounce up the lobby stairs of the Holston House Hotel, she seemed more excited to be there than he was.

ᘓᕒ

"She probably saw dollar signs," I said.

"I know she did," he said. "The next morning, I went to Mr. Stanley's office in Nashville. He had me sign a bunch of stuff with Gina in the room. I really didn't read any of it. He told me it was just standard licensing contracts, royalty agreements, that sort of thing. But I also signed something that made Gina my manager and gave her a commission on my earnings."

"That seems like a lot to throw at a twenty-year-old kid in one meeting," I said.

My father nodded in agreement. "I was just overwhelmed and very naïve. I didn't push back or ask questions about anything. I didn't want to look stupid."

ᘓᕒ

Two days after arriving in Nashville, and after Gina had taken him clothes shopping, Phillip found himself in a live room with studio musicians, technicians, and famed producer, Adam Fuller. After Phillip performed *Give Me a Reason* solo, as instructed, the group collaborated on a new arrangement for the song, one that would provide a richer, more emotional sound to compliment the lyrics. However, the technical nature of their creative discussion and the speed at which decisions were made reduced Phillip to an interested spectator. He had grown somewhat familiar with music theory jargon from his Sole Winners bandmates, but the musicians surrounding him in Nashville were in a different league.

In addition to Phillip's acoustic guitar, the new arrangement featured a violin, piano, drums, electric guitar, bass, and background vocals. After several hours of trial-and-error progress, mild arguments, and creative synergy led by Adam Fuller, the song that would soon make the artist called Walker Owens famous was ready for the recording process. By two-thirty the next morning, all thirteen tracks of the song had been recorded, ready to be mixed and mastered.

໑ঝ

"Did you like what they did with *Give Me a Reason*?" I asked.

"Oh, man, yes. To hear it after it was all mixed, left me speechless. I couldn't believe it was my song."

"Did you have to go through all that with every song on the album?"

"No, those were easy. All they needed was for me to add lead vocals. They did everything else."

"So, I'm guessing you didn't play the Sole Winners gig that Friday where you met Vallie."

"No, I was still in Nashville."

"OK, so…Vallie's out of the story."

"For now, yes."

"What do you mean?" I asked. "Does she time travel, too?"

"Don't be silly," my dad answered, "of course not."

"Dad, given what we've been talking about, I don't think that was a silly question."

My father laughed lightly. "I can see why you'd say that. But no, she didn't time travel."

"So, then Vallie's out for now, and you're back with Gina."

"That sums it up, yes."

"Not what you had in mind, was it?"

"No. Not at all."

"And you were officially Walker Owens."

"It took some getting used to, but that's what Mr. Stanley told everyone to call me. Even Gina."

"Wasn't Gina still in school during all this?"

"She was, thankfully. She had to go back to Columbia while we finished the album. It gave me time with Mr. Stanley to understand his plans for promoting it. But Gina had big plans of her own."

Julia approached us at the table and asked, "Mind if I steal the chessboard for a few minutes?"

"Go ahead, Julia," said my dad.

"Thanks," she said, taking the board from the table. "Gonna squeeze in a game while it's slow, if that's OK, Mr. Johnson."

"Absolutely, Julia," said my dad. "Have fun." He waited for a moment while Julia walked away, then said to me discreetly, "See that guy at the table over there? He's the one she's got a crush on."

"I know him," I said, watching as Julia joined him with the chessboard. "He teaches English Lit over at Hammond Academy. Dave or Dane…somebody."

"Good friend of yours?" my dad asked, grinning.

"Funny. No, I just got introduced to him one time at church. Seemed like a nice guy, though."

"That's good to know," he said. "Say, can we stop our story here for tonight? I need to be available to cover for Julia if we get busy."

"That's nice of you, Dad."

"What can I say? I'm a fan of true love."

NINETEEN

Fame

In between meetings with my dad, I was able to get a lunch date with Elizabeth. When I asked where she'd like to go, she said, "Anywhere but Groucho's." Trying to impress her, I suggested a rather eclectic – and much more expensive – restaurant downtown called Market on Main, or MOM as the regulars call it. Inside MOM, you could shop for bottles of wine or a variety of canned craft beers and sodas from their large refrigerators. Or buy to-go servings of prepared entrées, appetizers, and pasta salads from a glass display case. Or you could take a seat at the bar or dine-in at one of their many tables all in view of an open kitchen. We chose to sit on their large outdoor patio under an umbrella facing a performance stage where a lone college-age kid played acoustic guitar and tried to sing Third Eye Blind songs.

We spent our fifty minutes together, sipping iced tea and making slightly awkward small talk while we picked at our food. Neither of us drifted anywhere near relationship-oriented topics. But I did catch Elizabeth admiring an overtly happy couple sitting near us as if she were watching a scene from a sappy Hallmark movie. I knew that sentimental look; the question was how to make her look at me that way. Our lunch ended without an answer.

My dad and I met at his house on Wednesday night, again taking advantage of my mom's absence. We sat at the kitchen table and picked up where we left off.

"So, Dad, when we last talked, our hero, Walker Owens, had just finished recording his first album."

"Maybe *anti-hero* would be a better description," he said, greeting Pumpkin with a pat on the head as she joined us from the den.

"We won't call him that, but OK. So, tell me what happened next."

"Well, when I thought about writing this story myself, this is the part I was dreading."

"Why, Dad?"

His eyes dropped for a moment. "I kind of lost myself for a little while, there," he said, scratching his dog gently behind her ears. "Sometimes when you choose a path, you just have no idea what's waiting for you or how you'll handle it when it comes. And I'm not proud of some of the things I did. It's bad enough to talk about it, but I really didn't want to sit down and write about it. That's a whole other level of introspection I'd rather not deal with. That's one of the reasons I asked you to work with me on this."

"I'm happy to help, Dad. Why don't you just go with what you feel comfortable sharing, and I'll take it from there."

"OK, well, it started with *Give Me a Reason*."

$$\wp\!\!\sim\!\!\wp$$

Phillip's record label released *Give Me a Reason* as a lead single in advance of his first album, the eponymous *Walker Owens*. Heavily promoted and distributed, the song climbed to the top of *Billboard* magazine's Hot Country Singles chart in just four weeks, remaining there for two months. The single also had limited success on *Billboard's* Adult Contemporary and Mainstream Top 40 charts. Demand for interviews, live performances, and media appearances quickly followed.

With Gina unavailable for travel until her graduation in May, the label assigned a handler, at Phillip's expense, to manage his schedule. Manny Accardi, a former bouncer and doorman at the celebrity nightclub Studio 54 in Midtown Manhattan, told Phillip where to go, when to be there, what to wear, and, of increasing importance as time went on, when he'd had enough to drink.

Phillip's first large-scale concert appearance as Walker Owens took place in early spring of 1984 at the Houston Rodeo & Livestock Show in the Astrodome before 54,000 people. Shortly before climbing on stage, Phillip's bass player gave him a glass of iced Pepsi mixed with bourbon to help calm his nerves. He played a short four song set, opening with *Give Me a Reason*, before yielding the stage to country music legend George Strait.

Going forward, the Pepsi highball would become Phillip's anxiety panacea for all live performances before, during, and after his sets.

∽∾

"That's quite a jump to go from playing a bar in Columbia to the Astrodome."

"Tell me about it. It wasn't easy. But the guys the label sent out on tour with me were experienced musicians, so I leaned on them a good bit. Maybe too much."

"But what about Gina? You said you two got married."

"Oh, that," he said.

I laughed. "Yeah, that."

"Well, it was more of a wedding than a marriage."

"What do you mean?"

"After she graduated and started getting more involved with everything, the wedding was her idea to get publicity. *Walker Owens Weds College Sweetheart in Beach Ceremony on Nantucket*, that sort of thing. It was all for show. I never proposed to her or anything. She even hired a PR firm to promote it."

"Seriously?"

He nodded. "And it worked. A photographer and writer from *People* magazine were there. We made the cover."

"You made the cover of *People* magazine?"

"We did. But we never lived like married people. I was always on the road. She would show up for special appearances when media would be there, but other than that I didn't see her that much."

"Where was she?"

"Who knows? She got what she wanted from me. She was a rich celebrity's wife, manager of a successful recording artist with a big house in West Mead in Nashville. And she used my name to sign other acts." My dad paused as he reflected on his story.

I sat quietly and waited.

After a moment he shook his head and said solemnly, "I never wanted any of it."

"Any of what?" I asked.

"The whole celebrity thing. I just felt so…exposed all the time. After a while, I even got afraid to go out in public alone. I was scared someone would recognize me and think, 'Why is Walker Owens in a bar, or a store, or coffee shop by himself? Doesn't he have any friends?' Or even worse, they might come up and mob me like I was some puppy to have their picture taken with."

"But isn't that the fun of being a celebrity? All the attention?"

"Daniel, people have this idea of being famous, living an amazing life where everybody loves you. But it's not like that at all. You're an object. You're a product. A novelty. A photo-op. You have no idea what it's like to get up on a stage and play to thousands of people all staring at you, and then try to avoid them everywhere else you go. I just stayed in my hotel room all the time and drank myself to sleep every night. I felt like a prisoner."

❧

Phillip never desired fame. His interest in music flowed from the curious combination of sound and emotion he stumbled upon listening to his brother's country records. Once he learned to play, he found a freedom of expression unlike anything he'd ever experienced. His only desire was to share that experience with others. However, his success in that regard fueled the ambitions of those around him. While Gina and others profited, Phillip's own life spun quickly and quietly out of control.

❧

"But all that time," my dad said, "I kept thinking about Vallie and the night I had with her in my empty apartment in Columbia. Nothing I'd done since then came close to making me as happy. Not the money or the attention. I kicked myself every day for trading her for a music career. I just wanted to escape everything around me and be with her. So…I wrote a song about it. Can you go grab my guitar?" he asked. "It's in the hall closet again."

I trotted down the hallway to retrieve my father's guitar. My eagerness to hear him play again made me wonder if I was becoming a Walker Owens fan. I returned to the kitchen, handed him the guitar, and sat back and listened.

"This is called *Escape*," he said. "It's a ballad about just wanting to escape the life I was in if Vallie could just come with me. It goes like this."

> *Love help me through the fall*
> *My cup runs empty*
> *I swear I'd up and leave it all*
> *If you'll go with me*
> *Nothing else could be this daunting*
> *Time has come to leave 'em wanting*

> *Please light my way*
> *I just can't stay*
> *Come with me*

> *Time stole you away from me*
> *But someday I know*
> *My song will bring you back to me*
> *I'll go where you go*
> *I'd leave this dark and lonely cave*
> *If only I could be so brave*

> *Please guide my way*
> *I just can't stay*
> *Let's leave today*
> *Come with me*

> *Please tell me it wasn't just a dream*
> *Please tell me that you feel the same*
> *Please tell me you remember*

> *Please light my way*
> *I just can't stay*
> *Let's leave today*
> *Come with me*

"Dad, that's beautiful," I said, still having a hard time believing that was my dad in front of me.

"Thank you, Son. My record company loved it and didn't want to wait for another full album to release it. So, it came out as a stand-alone single."

"Did it do well?"

"It shot up the charts faster than *Give Me a Reason* and stayed at number one on the country charts for eleven weeks. It made it up to number nine on the pop charts, too. Just behind *Fresh* by Kool & the Gang. And it just so happens that while it was peaking, I played a concert at the New Mexico State Fair in Albuquerque. And guess who was there."

"Gouyen?"

"Guess again."

The door to the kitchen opened, and my mom entered with a large smile on her face.

"Hold that thought," my dad said to me.

"Guess who I just talked to," asked my mom in her singsong voice.

"It better not be Elizabeth," I said.

"Of course it was," she said joyfully.

"Mom, I asked you not to call her."

"I didn't. She called me."

"She did?"

"Hm-hmm."

"Why?"

"Oh, she just wanted to say hello and see how I was doing. Just catching up. You know, girl stuff."

"That's it?" I asked. "No conspiring or scheming this time?"

"Daniel," she said, "when are you going to trust your mother?"

I laughed. "I'll let you know when that happens, Mom."

"Very funny," she said, placing her purse on the counter. "So, what were you two boys talking about when I came in? You both looked guilty of something."

I looked at my dad.

"Sports," he said.

"That's right," I said, looking at my mother. "We were talking about sports. You know, guy stuff."

"Uh-huh," she said, narrowing her eyes at us.

"Well, I'd better be going," I said, standing up. "I'll see y'all later. Dad, just let me know when you want to talk more about sports and stuff."

"I will, Son. Goodnight."

As I headed out the door into the garage, I heard my mother say, "Sports, huh?"

TWENTY

Escape

Given the deliberate relationship subterfuge orchestrated by my mother a few weeks back, news of her call with Elizabeth had left me both suspicious and encouraged. Of course, any involvement by my mother fell into the suspicious category, no matter how benign it may appear on the surface. But the fact that Elizabeth had placed the call left me slightly hopeful. Perhaps my friendly lunch with her at Market on Main had softened her disappointment with me as a suitor. Maybe, as a next step, she'd be open to a nice dinner or even a night of bad karaoke at the Art Bar. But I didn't want to rush things, so I held off for a few days.

My dad came over to my house that Friday morning in mid-August for our writing session. School was starting for me the following week, so our meeting would be one of my last undistracted times with him for a while. After watching him play fetch with Bono in the backyard for a few minutes, I set up my laptop and legal pad on the kitchen table and we jumped right into our story.

My dad started us off. "I mentioned last time how I had gotten used to drinking Pepsi and bourbon to calm my nerves."

"The Pepsi highball, sure."

"Well, that night in Albuquerque," he said, hesitantly, "I overdid it a little bit. I didn't just drink more than usual before I went on, I had one of the stagehands keep me supplied during the concert. I kept a cup on a barstool next to me and would drink from it in between songs."

"Were you drunk on stage?" I asked.

"I wasn't like Elvis out there staggering around, forgetting the words to my own songs. But I definitely felt the effects, let's put it like that."

"I've got to say, Dad, it's a little weird hearing you talk about drinking. I've never seen you have a drink my entire life."

"Well, after this, you'll understand why."

"And the concert was at a state fair? With like, cows and Ferris wheels and cotton candy and stuff?"

"It was. We had a good-sized crowd, though. Nothing like the Astrodome, of course, but they had a large performance area for bands. George Strait was playing the next night, so at least I wasn't opening for him again. But for some reason, I was in a mood to drink. I guess I was just getting a little tired of everything."

"That's understandable."

"Still, the show started out fine. We were about four songs into our first set when I happened to look down to the third row and see Vallie looking back up at me."

"Vallie? In New Mexico? Are you sure it was her?"

"I was sure, believe me."

"What was she doing at the state fair in Albuquerque?"

"I had no idea. But there she was, holding up a sign that said, 'Escape with me!' Can you believe that?"

"What did you do?"

"I just froze. I couldn't believe it. We had just finished one of our songs called *Ain't My Night*, and my bass player had to come over and snap me out of my trance." My dad shook his head at himself.

"Did you say anything to her?" I asked.

"I did, but…"

"But what?"

"I just handled it all wrong. I don't know what got into me." After a brief moment, he added, "Actually, I know exactly what got into me."

With help from his bass guitarist, Phillip was able to take his eyes off Vallie. He turned his back to the crowd and took a long drink of his Pepsi and bourbon before setting the cup back on the barstool beside him. Regaining his composure, he gave a reassuring nod to his band and stepped up to the microphone. "I have a surprise for you tonight," he said to the crowd. "I'm guessing some of you have heard my song *Give Me a Reason*." Phillip took a step back and let the crowd's enthusiastic cheer build his confidence. "We'll play that for you in a bit," he continued. "What you may not know is that the girl who helped me write that song is here tonight." He glanced down at Vallie's unknowing, eager face as she held her sign high above her head. Over the crowd's polite applause, he said, "Wait, it gets better. I have a new single out called *Escape*." When the loud ovation died down, he added, "And I wrote that song about the same girl." Phillip looked directly at Vallie. "Her name is Vallie Ray."

Vallie dropped her sign and stood with her mouth hanging open.

"Would y'all like to meet her?" Phillip asked. With the crowd's approval, Phillip walked to the edge of the stage and extended his arm downward, his eyes locked on Vallie. He smiled and waved her forward.

In a zombie-like stupor, Vallie slipped past those standing around her and approached the stage. Two security guards helped her up as Phillip pulled her onto the platform. Offering her a seat on the barstool, he gave his drink to a stagehand who had run out to assist. "Bring me two backstage passes," Phillip told him. Turning to Vallie with a smile, Phillip said, "Hi!"

Vallie sat quietly smiling up at him, as some in the audience laughed at her inability to move or speak.

Turning to the crowd, Phillip introduced his next song. "This is a song I wrote about lost love. It's called *Escape*."

As Phillip began singing to Vallie, he swam in her wide, blue eyes, remembering her soft kiss that night in his apartment. And in the warmth of the spotlight, he felt alone with her once again. *Escape* was no longer just a song. He was speaking directly to her.

> *Please tell me it wasn't just a dream*
> *Please tell me that you feel the same*
> *Please tell me you remember*
>
> *Please light my way*
> *I just can't stay*
> *Let's leave today*
> *Come with me*

When the song ended, the full array of stage lights and loud applause reminded Phillip he was not alone with Vallie. The stagehand quickly appeared at Phillip's side with the passes, then ran off stage.

Phillip covered the microphone with his hand. "Come see me after the show," he said, handing the passes to Vallie. "The guards will show you how to find me."

Vallie remained speechless as Phillip waved for the stagehand to escort her back to her seat.

❦

"How did that feel?" I asked. "Having her with you on stage like that?"

"The whole time I was singing, I felt like I was floating. I'm sure the bourbon had something to do with that, but I started to think I had a chance to have everything. My career *and* Vallie."

"Did she come backstage after the show?"

"She did. But getting through the rest of the set was a challenge. I just wanted to hurry up and play through it so I could talk to her. And trying to manage the adrenalin and the excitement of all that, I kind of... overcompensated."

"Too much Pepsi and bourbon?" I asked.

With a look of chagrin, my dad said, "Yeah."

༺☙

Phillip paced anxiously around the dressing room waiting for Vallie to appear. This was his chance, he thought, to reclaim what Black Hole had taken away from him. He and Vallie had shared a connection once before, and he felt sure they could find it again. As he tilted his glass to finish the last of his drink, the room seemed to spin slowly around him. He decided against pouring another. A knock on the door snapped him to attention.

"Mr. Owens, you have two guests," a security guard said through the door.

"That's fine, thank you," he said, as the door opened.

Vallie entered, followed by a handsome young man, slightly older than Phillip.

"Hello, again," said Phillip to Vallie, giving her his best smile. "Thanks for sticking around."

"Hi, um...," started Vallie. "Walker Owens, this is my husband, Del Boykin."

Hearing the word *husband* changed Phillip's mood instantly. He ignored Del's offer of a handshake and kept his now scornful eyes on Vallie. "My name isn't Walker," he said.

"It's Phillip. Remember, Vallie? I called your room last year to tell you how much the label liked our song."

Vallie looked shocked. "That was you?"

Del turned quickly to Vallie. "Then you do know him!" he said accusingly.

Vallie took a step backward, shaking her head.

"And you must be the old boyfriend from Charleston," said Phillip throwing a dismissive scowl at Del.

"Vallie's my wife," asserted Del, his posture stiffening.

Phillip turned to Vallie. "So, he *was* the one, after all, huh, Vallie?"

"How did you—" Vallie stopped herself midsentence.

"What does he mean by that?" asked Del, glaring at Vallie.

Vallie shook her head. "I don't know. I—"

"It was just one night, Del," added Phillip, with a sly grin. "Nothing to worry about."

"You cheated on me with this guy?"

"No! He's lying. I have no idea what he's talking about!"

"This is why you're so crazy about him?"

"No! I like his music, that's all! Del, I swear!"

Del turned and stormed out of the dressing room, much to Phillip's delight.

Vallie started after him, but turned back to Phillip and shouted, "You bastard! I hate you!"

༒

"When Vallie said that to me and slammed the door behind her, something inside me just broke. I knew I would never be able to get that out of my head. I had hurt the one person I cared about. And maybe even ruined her marriage. All because I felt like being a cocky jerk."

"Is that why you stopped drinking?"

"Yes, but I wasn't quite done with it, yet."

"There's more?"

"There is, but why don't we save it for next time?" he said. "I need to go check on the café."

"You like to leave me hanging, don't you?"

My father smiled as he pushed away from the table. "It's just the writer in me, I guess."

Anxious to keep our project moving forward, I asked, "Would you mind coming back over tomorrow morning, Dad? Say ten o'clock?"

"Sure. Would you like me to bring some blueberry scones from the café?"

"In that case, make it nine o'clock. I don't think I could wait until ten for your scones. And could you bring a couple for Elizabeth? She loves those."

"Now you're thinking, Son. I'll see you tomorrow."

TWENTY-ONE

Destiny

I woke up Saturday thinking about blueberry scones from my dad's cafe. Yes, they were good to eat, all buttery, crumbly, and fruity, but they also made a good excuse to see Elizabeth. She was working a twelve-hour shift at the hospital that day, and I planned to surprise her with a few scones later that morning. Shortly after nine o'clock, my dad arrived at my house with a half dozen. I ate one and saved the rest for Elizabeth. Not that she would eat five by herself, but she could share them with her team at the hospital, who would then have to say nice things about her boyfriend. It was a perfect plan.

"How do you keep from eating all these, yourself?" I asked my dad as I enjoyed the last few crumbs off my plate.

"They're not food to me," he said. "They're just revenue-generating inventory."

I laughed at my inability to relate. "That's a mental trick I'm glad I don't have to worry about," I said, clearing a space on the table for my laptop, phone, and notepad. "Are you ready to get started?"

"I'm ready," he said. "We're getting close to the end, you know."

"That's exciting," I said, tapping my phone to start recording. "Where did we leave things yesterday?"

"I think Vallie had just left my dressing room after the concert."

"Oh, that's right. The *bastard, I hate you* comment."

163

"Thanks for the reminder."

"So, what did you do after that?"

"Well, I wanted to be alone for a little while to think, but that was impossible with people coming in and out. So, I grabbed a bottle of whiskey from our storage bin and asked my limo driver if I could borrow his keys so I could put something in his trunk. And then I got on the road to Santa Rosa."

"In the limo?"

"Yep."

The grin on my father's face made me seek clarification on one minor detail. "Please tell me your driver took you there."

His grin gave way to a full smile. "Nope. I stole the limo."

"You stole the limo," I repeated.

"Hm-hmm," he said, trying unsuccessfully to suppress his laughter. "My driver was running after me, waving his arms in the air. I needed a laugh right about then, so I really enjoyed seeing that in the rearview mirror."

I struggled to find an appropriate response to that but failed. "Dad, how do you want me to write about that?"

"Just like it happened, how else?"

"That you got drunk and stole a car."

"Something like that, sure. With a little more detail of course."

I sat shaking my head subtly while I made a few notes on my legal pad. First time travel, then drinking, and now car theft. What other dark secrets waited for me, I wondered.

"Look, I know what you're thinking," he said, "but if things worked out with Black Hole the way I hoped they would, the driver would never know the difference. That makes sense, doesn't it?"

"I suppose there's logic in there somewhere," I said with a shrug as I considered my writing task. "I'll think of something."

"So, anyway, it was between three and four in the morning by the time I got to Santa Rosa. And then it took me a little while to find the trail off the highway to Black Hole."

My dad seemed to be enjoying himself, but the story was suddenly moving faster than my ability to process it. I realized he was telling me *what* happened without telling me *why* it happened. So, I said, "Dad, let's slow it down just a bit. Tell me what was going on in your head around that time. I get that you were upset about Vallie, but why Black Hole again? What made you go back out there?"

In his eyes, I saw a glimpse of the pain he had experienced that night in Albuquerque. "I guess I can thank Manny for that," he said.

ৎ৵৵

Phillip stood motionless, staring at the closed door. The words "I hate you" floated with the bourbon through his stunned mind. But his time alone to contemplate Vallie's harsh exit ended quickly with a parade of rowdy tour personnel, band members, and groupies flowing in and out of the room. Frustrated with the sudden lack of privacy, Phillip escaped past them into the hallway, grabbing a bottle of whiskey on his way out. Unsure where he was headed, he staggered down the backstage corridor to find his handler, Manny, sitting in one of two chairs by the exit.

"Guarding the door, Manny?" asked Phillip, sarcastically.

"Old habits die hard," joked Manny. Pointing to the bottle in Phillip's hand, he asked, "Where are you headed?"

"Oh, just outside, you know."

"I think you've had enough for one night, don't you?"

"No, not with the night I've had."

"What's wrong? The show went well. Inviting that girl on stage was a nice touch."

"That girl…," said Phillip, shaking his head. "Mind if I sit down?"

"Have a seat."

Phillip plopped down in the chair. He felt small sitting next to Manny, who looked intimidating without effort. His military-style haircut, dark suit, and white dress shirt with no tie, fitted over his large frame gave the appearance of a hitman or secret service agent. Personal conversations had not been a part of their business relationship. But Phillip needed a friend at that moment, and Manny would have to do.

"Manny, have you ever had a girl you really wanted to be with, but just couldn't?"

Phillip watched Manny turn his head and study him for a moment. He expected the usual remark about his alcohol consumption or the need to get him back to his hotel room. But Manny's answer surprised him.

"When I worked at Studio 54," began Manny, "I bet I fell in love ten or fifteen times every night."

"Really?" asked Phillip, genuinely shocked.

Manny gave a rare smile as he nodded. "The number of beautiful women who wanted to get in that place – and I had to say no to a lot of them – would blow your mind. And I won't even tell you what some of them offered to do if I just let them in."

"Did you ever, you know…"

"What? Take them up on it? No. That would be unprofessional. I had a job to do. Besides, I knew it wasn't me they wanted. They just wanted to use me."

"That sounds familiar," said Phillip, grimly.

"I'm guessing by that you mean Gina."

"Yeah," said Phillip. "That's been her MO since day one. It just took me a while to realize it."

"I figured that out the first time I saw you two together."

"Seriously?"

"Trust me. I can spot a woman like that a mile away. But hey, look at the bright side. She's never around." Manny elbowed Phillip as they shared a laugh. "But I'm guessing the girl you asked me about isn't Gina."

"No, it's not."

"Was it the girl on stage?" guessed Manny.

"Yeah. Vallie. I met her in college. But then the whole record deal thing happened, and I lost her. Now she's married and hates my guts."

"Why do you think she hates you?"

"Well for starters, she said, 'I hate you.'"

Manny chuckled. "OK, that's certainly a tip-off."

"Yeah. But I deserved it," said Phillip. "This whole Walker Owens thing..."

"Maybe that's the problem," suggested Manny.

Phillip looked up at him. "What do you mean?"

"Look, Walker—"

"You can call me Phillip."

"All right, Phillip. I was just going to say that I've seen a lot of people in your shoes lose themselves. Some to drugs and alcohol. Some to their own egos. Some to both. Fame changes people. So, let me ask you, Phillip, did this girl like you before you made it big?"

"Yes. She really did. It was amazing."

"And now she hates you."

"Yep."

Manny raised an eyebrow and said, "Then do the math."

In that instant, Phillip knew where and who he wanted to be. And the answer wasn't hotel rooms, arenas, and Walker Owens. He wanted to go home. To a time when he was simply Phillip Johnson. More than anything, he wanted to erase the pain he had just caused Vallie. And he knew what he had to do.

"Have you seen our limo driver?" Phillip asked.

"I think he's outside," said Manny.

"I'll be right back."

Phillip grabbed his bottle of whiskey from the floor, opened the door, and walked outside. His driver leaned against the limo under a lamppost as he talked with two women. Phillip approached casually. "Hey, James, can I borrow your keys for a sec? Manny wants to put some things in the trunk."

"Sure," said James, tossing the keys to Phillip.

"Can you give Manny a hand?" asked Phillip. "He's just inside the door, there."

James excused himself from his conversation and started toward the building. Phillip waited until James reached the door, then ran to the driver's side of the limo and jumped in. Turning the keys in the ignition, he looked back to see James sprinting toward the car. Phillip put the limo in drive, stepped on the gas, and spun the tires in the dirt as he sped away. He glanced in the rearview mirror and laughed heartily at the sight of James running through the dust waving his arms over his head. Phillip's next stop was Santa Rosa.

§∞§

"Did you drive the limo on the horse trail?" I asked my dad.

"I did," he said. "And it was a lot smoother drive than in my car, believe me. Which is good, because I'd been sipping on that bottle of whiskey all the way from Albuquerque. It's a wonder I made it at all."

§∞§

Phillip took a seat atop the canyon wall overlooking the Pecos River. He was in no hurry. While still dark, the terrain around him was lit by a star-filled sky and a nearly full moon sliding slowly below the western horizon. Phillip nursed his bottle of whiskey while giving serious, if not inebriated, thought to the direction of his life. He had been down the same path twice, the fork in the road each time being his audition. One event, two unique destinies.

"My destiny," he said to himself with sarcastic, over-played drama. "Whatever."

He rolled over to his hands and knees, pushed himself to his feet, and began a stumbling descent to the river below. Once on the canyon bottom, he stepped into the water and splashed toward Black Hole. "Third time's the charm," he said with a giggle.

Staggering through the shallows, Phillip approached the cave entrance. The smell of sulfur wasn't as strong as he remembered, but the whiskey coursing through his veins may have dulled his senses. A small grey fox sat atop the mouth of the cave eying his movements in the dim early morning light. "What are you looking at?" Phillip slurred at the fox. He removed the cowboy hat from his head, let it fall to the ground, and pointed to the cave. "You know, they should put up a warning sign that says, 'This cave can be dangerous to your love life.'" He laughed at his own joke as the animal's blank stare remained fixed upon him. Gathering himself, and with deliberate intention, he said, "OK, let's do this." Phillip took his last sip of whiskey, tossed the bottle into the river, and meandered toward the cave. "So much for Walker Owens," he said and disappeared into the darkness.

∽◌⌒

"Let me ask it right this time," I said, "*When* did you wake up?"

"Same as last time," said my dad. "I was in my five-dollar motel room in Santa Rosa. Completely sober."

"That was my next question," I said, laughing. "How about your car? Was it across the street at the garage?"

"Yep, just like the last two times. But this time, after I paid for it, I just drove home."

"You didn't go to your audition?"

"No." My dad sat quietly for a moment, reflecting on his story. "You know, at some point," he said, "I might have had dreams about being another George Jones or Earl Thomas Conley or George Strait. And I got a little taste of that as Walker Owens. But sometimes dreams are better than reality. So, I decided to just keep my dreams as dreams."

His story finally matched everything my mother had told me. "What about your last gig with the Sole Winners?" I asked. "Did you meet Vallie again?"

Before my dad could answer, his phone rang. I waited patiently as he talked to one of his employees.

"I'm sorry, Son, I have to head back to the café."

"Is everything OK?"

"Just a problem with this week's order. My delivery guy is there, and I need to catch him before he leaves. Can we pick it up again later?"

"Sure, Dad. And thanks again for the scones."

"Any time. Good luck with Elizabeth."

After my dad left, I hopped in the shower and got dressed. By the time I got to the hospital to find Elizabeth, it was close to lunchtime and a little late for breakfast scones. But I hoped to get points for trying. As I entered the hospital lobby, my phone vibrated in my pocket. A quick look told me my mother was calling. She must have heard I was taking scones to Elizabeth and wanted an update. I ignored the call, but it vibrated again as soon as I returned it to my pocket. So, I sighed and answered.

"Hey, Mom."

"Daniel, where are you?"

"I'm at the hospital, why?"

"Oh, good, you're already there. I'm headed that way right now."

"Mom, I think I can deliver scones without you."

"What?"

"The scones for Elizabeth. I've got it, Mom, don't worry."

"Daniel, your father's had a stroke."

TWENTY-TWO

Time

As I waited impatiently for the slowest elevator on the planet to reach the third floor of the hospital, I had a moment to consider the situation. It was all my fault, I decided. If I had spent as much time worrying about my dad's health as I did stupid little things like delivering blueberry scones to Elizabeth, maybe he wouldn't be a patient in the same hospital. When the elevator doors finally opened, I sped down the hallway toward post-op, where Elizabeth worked. She happened to be standing at the nurses' station and saw me coming. Her smile quickly faded as she read the expression on my face.

"My dad's had a stroke," I said, placing the bag of scones on the counter.

"Where is he?" she asked, quickly.

"He's here somewhere. My mother called and said she's on her way. That's all I know."

Elizabeth ran around the counter and sat down in front of a computer. "Do you know if he was conscious when he came in?" she asked.

"I don't know."

"They may have listed him with a random name and number until they can get an ID, but let's see," she said, typing. She explained that if he wasn't still in the emergency room, he was most likely in the Neuro ICU. "Here he is," she said, looking at the screen. "He's upstairs. Come on, I'll go with you."

173

As we hurried down the hall toward the elevator, she asked, "What was in the bag?"

"Oh, those are scones from my dad's café," I said, lacking the enthusiasm I had for them a short while ago. "I thought you and your team might enjoy them."

"That was sweet," she said, pushing the elevator up button on the wall. Then as an afterthought, she asked, "You thought to get those after your dad had a stroke?"

"What? No, those were from this morning. He brought them to my house with a few extra for you."

"So, you saw him just this morning? How was he?"

"He was totally fine. Then a couple hours later, this."

We hopped on the elevator and Elizabeth pushed the ninth-floor button. The doors closed with just the two of us inside. The slow ride up felt awkward. I realized we hadn't been alone for weeks. She kept her eyes on the display showing which floors we were passing, and I quietly wondered what we were going to find when the doors finally opened.

Once out of the elevator, Elizabeth told me to wait there while she went to check on things. I took the opportunity to text my mother and let her know where we were. After a brief discussion with a nurse down the hall, Elizabeth stuck her head into a curtain-draped room, then waved me toward her. I walked as fast as I could without running, but what I saw when I got there was startling.

I didn't expect my father to be awake. But there he was, lying in a bed fully conscious, his face strangely contorted and his eyes wide open, darting with confusion in all directions. He didn't acknowledge my presence in any discernable way. An attending physician stood looking at his vital signs on the display above his bed, while a nurse adjusted the IV bag hanging beside him.

"I have to go back downstairs," Elizabeth said, her eyes beginning to fill. "Please keep me updated."

"Are you his son?" the doctor asked as Elizabeth hurried away.

"Yes, sir. How is he?"

"Your father's had an acute ischemic stroke."

"I'm sorry; what is that?"

"He's experienced a left carotid terminus occlusion."

That didn't help, either. So, I said, "And that means…"

"One of the two main arteries to his brain was blocked by a blood clot," he explained.

"Oh, got it," I said. "But he's going to be all right, isn't he?"

"As far as any long-term damage to his brain, it's hard to say at this point. We have him on intravenous fibrinolysis, which should prevent any more damage and hopefully restore some blood flow to the affected part of his brain."

"Why isn't he asleep or sedated?" I asked, looking at my dad.

"Time is the critical factor in these situations, Mr. Johnson. Every second matters. We couldn't risk delaying his treatment to administer general anesthesia. But he's under conscious sedation. Don't worry, he's not in any physical discomfort."

The doctor excused himself and left the room, followed by the nurse, who pushed the curtain to one side, leaving the room open to the hallway. As I stood there alone with my father, it was hard to accept that he was the same person I had seen earlier that morning. I leaned over and placed my hand on his arm. "Dad?" I said, hopefully. His wide eyes turned quickly to me as he made unintelligible, but emphatic sounds with his mouth. "It's OK, Dad. It's OK. I'm here. And Mom's on her way. You're going to be all right, OK? You're going to be all right. I promise." I let go of his arm and hoped that I wasn't lying to him.

Checking my phone, I saw where my mother had replied to my text, but as I began typing, she walked into the room. She gave me a silent hug, then moved to my father's side and grabbed his hand.

"What did they say?" she asked, wiping tears from her eyes as she looked down at him. "Have you talked to a doctor?"

"I just did. They're treating him with the IV for blood clots."

"Did they say if he'll be OK?" she asked hopefully.

"He said it's too early to tell."

She turned to my dad, leaned down, and kissed him on his cheek, his eyes still moving randomly around the room. "I love you," she whispered.

"Mom, how did this happen?"

Wiping her cheeks with a tissue from her purse, she said, "All I know is that he was in the café, and Julia said he started complaining of a sudden headache and had to sit down. Then he started slurring his speech and couldn't stand up. So, she called an ambulance. I'm so glad she was there, Daniel. She said the other two girls working with her laughed at him. They thought it was funny."

"That kind of makes me angry," I said.

"They're kids, honey, what do you expect?"

I shook my head. "This is all my fault."

"No, it's not your fault," she said, squeezing my hand. "If your father wasn't such a...stubborn mule about going to the doctor, we might have had time to prevent this." She paused as she looked down at him. In a broken voice, she added, "But what's done is done. We just have to hope he'll recover and learn a lesson from all this."

With my mother's words, a thought began forming in my mind until it crashed over me like a ten-foot wave. My mouth dropped open as I took a step back. "Mom, would you excuse me for a second?"

"Where are you going?"

"I'll be right back."

I hurried down the hallway, past the elevator, and ran down six flights of stairs. Back on Elizabeth's floor, I headed toward the nurses' station at the end of the hall but saw her in a room next to a patient's bed. I barged right in.

"Elizabeth, I have to ask you a question."

"Daniel, you can't just walk in here while I'm—"

"If my father had started taking antiplatelets a few weeks ago, could they have prevented this?"

"Well, maybe, but—"

"That's all I needed to know," I said and turned toward the door.

"Where are you going?" I heard her say behind me.

"New Mexico!" I shouted from the hallway.

TWENTY-THREE

Faith

Desperation can make you believe and do crazy things sometimes. My decision to leave the hospital and drive straight to the airport is a prime example. Wanting to believe my father's Black Hole story, I planned to go back in time and prevent his stroke from happening. That sounds totally ridiculous, I know, but it is what I was thinking when I left. If his story proved to be just a convincing work of fiction, I would have some serious explaining to do when I returned home. Not to mention a $1,629 airline charge on my credit card.

Once at the airport, I found it was hard to get to Albuquerque from Columbia. So, I flew into Santa Fe, about a hundred miles north of Santa Rosa. My flight landed just before ten o'clock that night, and I was able to get a car rental for the drive south. It was almost midnight when I took the exit off I-40 for Santa Rosa. My phone had been blowing up with calls and text messages from my mother and Elizabeth, but I chose to ignore them. There was no way to explain what I was doing, and silence felt easier on my conscience than inventing a lie.

Driving into Santa Rosa on Route 66, the town was very different than what my father had described, offering a lot more than just a truck stop and a bar. There were houses and banks and places to eat. And instead of a lone five-dollar-a-night motel, I saw signs for Super 8 and Days Inn. I admit that seeing the reality of Santa Rosa cast some doubt in my mind about my father's time there. But it had been almost forty years since his last visit, I reasoned. Besides, I was way past second-guessing my purpose for being there.

Using Google Maps on my phone, I was able to find my way to a trail that led off Highway 91 into the desert toward the Pecos River. It seemed more like a normal dirt road than a horse trail, so I drove on it with relative ease. I followed the road until it reached a dead-end at a group of small trees and large rocks. According to the terrain view in Maps, it was just a short walk from there to the river canyon.

Since both of my father's visits to Black Hole happened shortly before dawn, I wanted to wait a little while before I ventured into the cave. Although, it seemed like a good idea to make sure there was, in fact, a cave down there. So, I stepped out of my rented Nissan Versa and walked carefully toward the canyon. It was dark, but the light from the clear night sky lit my surroundings fairly well, just as my father described. Still, I felt the need to use my phone light to scout for rattlesnakes.

After about a hundred yards or so, I arrived at the top of the canyon. My dad had done such a good job describing his experience, my view had a familiar feel. Just as he did, I took a seat on a large boulder and looked down on the Pecos. And sure enough, at the base of the canyon across the river sat a dark, circular shadow.

I sat there for a while on the rock, thinking about the last thirteen hours of my life. I had run out of the hospital leaving my mother alone in a time of crisis, wondering where I went. I had ignored all attempts to reach me from the people I love, adding to their pain and worry. And I had spent a lot of money I really didn't have. I did all that because I love my dad. And I would do anything to save him, even if it meant putting my faith in his highly unlikely, physically improbable, hard-to-believe time travel story. So, there I was. Gazing down at what I sincerely hoped was the mystical Black Hole, ready to take my chances.

After a short nap in the car, my phone alarm woke me at five o'clock. I shook the sleep from my head, got out of the car, and headed back to the canyon. After sliding down the hill to the bottom, I began wading across the river. While my dad had described it as being ankle-deep and easy to cross, the water was moving a good bit faster than I expected and rose to my knees. Nevertheless, I made it to the other side and approached the mouth of the cave.

The only instruction I remembered from my dad's story was to walk a straight path. But as I stood before the entrance staring into the darkness, my feet weren't moving. The mental image of me strolling into the cave and waking up a family of wolves held me captive. Trying hard to clear my head, I thought of my dad lying in that hospital bed looking confused and helpless. And I remembered my promise that he would be OK. It was all the motivation I needed. After taking a deep breath, I stepped forward. The last thought I remember as I entered the darkness was a fear of waking up in a five-dollar-a-night motel room in 1983.

TWENTY-FOUR

String Theory

My eyes opened to the sound of a bird chirping loudly outside my bedroom window. I found myself lying on my side, my head resting comfortably on my pillow with Bono sound asleep at my feet. The clock on my nightstand read 6:33 AM. My phone lay beside the clock, having charged overnight. While I felt a general sense of surreal confusion, it seemed to be fading quickly. Perhaps the latent guilt and trauma of my father's stroke had fueled a vivid early morning dream about flying to New Mexico and entering Black Hole. I allowed myself a small laugh, reached for my phone, and tapped the screen. The date read Thursday, July 28th. I had never yelled out of shock before, but I did then. Poor Bono flew off the bed and ran out of the room.

I quickly swiped up to check my text messages. The last message was from my father on July 27th about meeting again that Friday. Gone were the barrage of messages and voice mails from my mother and Elizabeth. I took a quick look at my voice memos. The last recorded session with my dad was also from Wednesday the 27th. I pushed myself upright against my headboard. What was happening?

I sat there, stunned, considering the real possibility that I had just woken up a little over two weeks *before* my father's stroke. Had I really traveled in time? I looked at my phone again, opened the browser, and typed, "today's date" in the search bar. Google returned Thursday, July 28th. My phone wasn't lying. It really was the twenty-eighth of July. I had traveled in time. My dad's story of Walker Owens, Gina, and Vallie was real. It took me a few minutes to process all that, but at some point, my attention returned to my main concern: my dad.

Not that I understood or had any control over how Black Hole worked, but I felt a little pressed for time with only sixteen days until my dad's stroke. Another week would have been nice. As it was, I would need help getting him in to see a doctor quickly. And Elizabeth was my best hope. If she would agree to help me, that is.

I then realized *when* I was in the context of all things Elizabeth. On the 28th of last month – actually, it was *this* month now – we were still on our "fake break" orchestrated by my mother. And, most importantly, I was still a day away from my idiotic, spontaneous proposal at Groucho's. That meant she wasn't all that mad at me, yet. I just had to make up for ignoring her for three weeks.

I decided to send her a quick text asking for help in getting an appointment for my dad. I started a new message but stopped typing before I even finished the first sentence. "What am I doing?" I said out loud as I sat there in bed. Not only did I have a second chance to help my father, but I could also make things right with Elizabeth. With that in mind, I sent her the following carefully worded text.

> Hey there! I bet you were wondering if you'd hear from me again. ☺ I wasn't ghosting you, I promise. I was just trying to respect your desire for a little space. But I've missed you terribly. The break has made me realize how much I love you and how much I value our relationship. Do you think it would be possible for us to have lunch tomorrow? I'd love to see you.

Hey! I was beginning to wonder! I've missed
you, too. And I'm sorry for this whole break
business. Let's meet at Groucho's tomorrow.
I can do 11:30 if that works for you.

Perfect! I can't wait to see you! By the way,
you were 100% right about my dad. He does
need to see a doctor asap to get on
antiplatelets. Do you have any contacts that
could see him today or tomorrow?

Yikes! That might be difficult. Let me see
what I can do. Thanks for reaching out!
I've been hoping you would.

You're the best! See you tomorrow!

I sat with my phone in my hand unsure what I should do next. I had the rest of the day to live over again, but I couldn't remember anything important happening that Thursday the first go-round. So, since Black Hole had erased two weeks' worth of writing from my computer, I decided to spend the day recapturing from memory as much of my dad's story as I could.

Around four o'clock in the afternoon, I received a text from Elizabeth.

Got your dad an appointment with Dr.
Rayborne tomorrow morning at 8:00. She's
in the medical park next to the hospital.
Just make sure you get there on time. She's
going to see him first. Hope that works!

Thank you!! See you tomorrow at
Groucho's!

My sleep that night was interrupted by the frequent thought that what I was experiencing wasn't really happening. Everything seemed real enough, but as I bounced back and forth between sleep and wakeful anxiety, I had thoughts of it all being a dream. The concept still seemed ridiculous: time travel. But when I realized my dreams were about me having a dream that

I had traveled in time, I finally just gave up on sleep and got out of bed. It was four o'clock in the morning.

I worked on my father's story until I left for my parents' house at seven-thirty. On the drive over, I lectured myself about being non-negotiable with my dad. One way or the other, he was going to the doctor's office with me. I pulled into their driveway, got out, and walked into their house like a man on a mission. My dad liked to get up early, and I was counting on him being ready for the day when I got there. Sure enough, he was sitting by himself at the kitchen table, fully dressed, reading the paper and drinking coffee.

"Well, hey, Son," he said as I entered without saying hello. "What brings you out this early in the morning?"

"Dad, I need you to come with me."

He smiled and played along. "Where are we going?"

"Elizabeth got you an appointment with a neurologist. But we have to go right now. It's at eight o'clock."

'Son, I've already told you, I don't need to see a doctor."

Before I explained further, I needed to know if my mother could hear our conversation. "Where is Mom?" I asked.

"She's in the shower."

"All right," I said, ready to press forward. "Dad, do you know where I was yesterday?"

"You mean after you left the café?" he asked.

Confused about the whole multiple timeline thing, I said, "How do I explain this…OK, *my* yesterday, I was in Santa Rosa, New Mexico."

He stared at me for a moment with a quizzical look on his face but said nothing.

"Dad, two weeks from tomorrow, you're going to have a stroke. A bad one. You'll be in the hospital and won't be able to speak or anything. And you may not even recover."

"And how do you know all that?"

"Because to me, it's already happened. I saw you in the hospital."

He studied the serious look on my face. "You've been to Black Hole, haven't you?" he asked.

"Yes, Dad, I have. You told me all about it before your stroke happened."

I waited for a response, but he just looked down and said nothing.

"So, come on," I said. "Let's go. I'm not taking no for an answer this time."

He gave me a slight smile and said, "So, you decided to believe my story, after all."

"Obviously," I said, holding my arms out in exasperation. "Now let's go."

And that was all it took. He stood up from the table, said, "Give me one sec," and walked down the hallway toward his bedroom. A moment later, he returned. "I just had to let your mother know where we were going. I think you made her day."

As I backed the car out of his driveway, my dad asked, "So, how far had we gotten in the story before you left for Santa Rosa?"

I began driving slowly through his neighborhood and said, "You had played your concert in Albuquerque, then you went to Black Hole and came back home instead of going to your audition. That's as far as we got."

"I see. We're almost done then."

"Well, not really. I need your help recapturing everything we talked about between now and then. All my notes are gone."

"That's not a problem," he said. "Since you've already heard it once, it shouldn't take too long to redo." He paused and looked out the windshield for a moment, then asked, "So, have you given any thought, yet, to your own situation?"

"My situation? What do you mean?"

"Aside from taking me to the doctor, what else could you do differently over the next two weeks that really matters?"

My thoughts jumped straight to Elizabeth. "Well, I hadn't told you this before, but when I have lunch with Elizabeth today at Groucho's, the first time I asked her to marry me."

"And you didn't tell us about it?"

"No. She wanted to hold off on that."

"But she said yes, right?"

"Well, technically. But she didn't take it too well."

"Why not?"

"Let's just say she was hoping for a more romantic engagement proposal. And I really let her down."

"Well?" he asked expectantly.

"Well, what?"

"Now's your chance to fix that."

My dad had a good point, but I didn't trust my own romantic instincts, for good reason, and was hesitant to go down that path again. But he had offered to help me in that regard twice before without being specific, so it seemed like a good time to find out what he meant. "Just how would you suggest I do that?"

"If you really want to do it right," he said, "sing to her."

"Sing to her? That's your department, Dad, not mine."

"Oh, come on; it's not hard. I'm telling you, if you look her in the eyes and sing a love song to her, I promise you'll sweep her off her feet. You saw your mom on her birthday. And that was just a little number I wrote in about ten minutes."

"I can't write songs, Dad. Get real."

"Does Elizabeth have a favorite song? A love song that she really likes?"

I had to think on that for a minute, but I had a good story that seemed to answer his question. "Do you remember when I was bartending at night to help save money to buy a house?" I began.

"Sure, at the fancy steak place on Main Street."

"Right. That's where I first met Elizabeth. She came in one night with a friend of hers named Janet, and they sat at the bar. I served them a couple of rounds of margaritas and chatted with them while they drank. I also slipped them some free breadsticks so they wouldn't be drinking on an empty stomach. And then a song came on our sound system that Elizabeth really liked, and she and Janet started singing along with it."

"Out loud?"

I nodded. "They were getting a little tipsy, so they weren't being shy about it. And Elizabeth was so beautiful, oh my gosh. They were really having a good time until my manager came over. He told them they were disturbing our dinner guests and to stop singing or he'd ask them to leave. He was kind of a jerk about it."

"Did they stop?"

"They did, but I could tell they were embarrassed. I felt bad about it, so when the next chorus came up, I started singing out loud, pretending to really get into it."

"I bet they liked that."

"They loved it. They started singing along with me. Everybody in the whole place was looking at us. Some were laughing or smiling, but I could tell some people weren't happy about it at all."

"I'm guessing your manager asked the girls to leave."

"Actually, he told all three of us to leave. He fired me."

"Right then?"

"Yep."

"You never told me you got fired."

"It was just a bartender job, who cares? But since the girls felt responsible for getting me fired, they invited me to hang out with them the rest of the night. After that, Elizabeth and I started dating."

"Do you remember the song that got you in trouble?"

"Sure. It was *I'll Be* by Edwin McCain."

"That's it, then."

"What's it?"

"If you really want to win her over, sing that song to her."

"No way," I said, with a laugh. "That would be so awkward."

"Not if you do it right," he said. "I tell you what, let me look into a few things for you."

Once again, I had no idea what he meant by that, but we had just arrived at the doctor's office and had to table our discussion. We walked into the lobby to find five or six people already waiting. But after my dad introduced himself to the nurse at the check-in window, she invited him to go on back. The doctor was ready for him, she said.

I took a seat and picked up the latest *Sports Illustrated* to occupy my time. But before I could find a decent article to read, my dad came back out with a prescription in his hand. The nurse said there was no charge. Their only request was that he schedule an appointment within the next two weeks for a full evaluation. Elizabeth must have pulled some serious strings. I was impressed.

As I drove my dad to Walgreens to get his prescription filled, our conversation had nothing to do with time travel, engagement proposals, or dementia. We just talked and laughed about an episode of *Seinfeld* called "The Boyfriend" that he had seen recently and enjoyed the ride as father and son. I think we both needed that.

TWENTY-FIVE

Make it Right

When my father and I returned from our trip to the doctor, my mother greeted us in the kitchen. Upon seeing his medication and learning he'd return for another appointment in two weeks, she hugged both of us. I glanced at my father and noticed the same expression I saw when he had finished serenading my mother on her birthday. He knew he had just done something to make her happy. And that made him happy. I only hoped we had done it soon enough to make a difference.

With my dad taken care of for the time being, I left their house shortly after eleven with nothing but Elizabeth on my mind. As I drove back downtown toward Groucho's, I wondered how the script might be different than our last lunch there. Would she be in the same anxious mood? Would she get mad at me again? Would they forget to leave the bacon off her sandwich? And this time, since I was the one who initiated our lunch date – and had already claimed to have learned my lesson from our break – would she still feel compelled to confess her backroom liaison with my mother?

I decided to play things a little differently and arrive for our lunch date a few minutes after eleven-thirty. As I passed the front of Groucho's on the sidewalk, I could see her through the plate glass window already sitting at our usual table. She saw me, smiled, and waved. So far, so good, I thought as I entered through the front door. I made my way to our table and took a seat across from her.

"I already ordered for us," she said before I could say anything.

"Did you tell her no bacon on your sandwich?"

"Of course."

"Just making sure. Sometimes they forget."

"They've never gotten it wrong before," she said. "Kayla takes good care of us."

"Well, we'll see," I said, knowingly. "Thanks for meeting me for lunch."

"Thanks for asking," she said. "How did things go with Dr. Rayborne this morning? Did your dad get in to see her OK?"

"Yeah, everything went great. He's on meds now, and you made it really easy for us. Thank you so much."

"Dr. Rayborne is really nice. I play tennis with her sometimes."

"Ah, that explains it. I was wondering how we got in and out of her office so fast."

She looked down for a moment, then said, "Daniel, I've been wanting to talk with you about something."

Here it comes, I thought. "Sure, go ahead."

"I just feel like I need to be honest with you. So, promise you won't get mad at me."

"I promise."

"Or your mother," she added sheepishly, just as before.

"I promise. You both have full amnesty."

"Well, this whole taking a break thing was something your mom and I came up with." She paused and gave me an expectant look.

"Let me guess," I said casually. "You were hoping it would motivate me to take the next step in our relationship. You know, absence makes the heart grow fonder and all that."

"Exactly," she said, looking a bit stunned. "Did your mother tell you this already?"

"No," I answered honestly.

"Then how did you know all that?"

I smiled and said, "Call it gifted insight."

She narrowed her eyes at me and said, "Hmm…strange."

"Anyway, it worked, didn't it?" I offered. "You should be happy."

A bit suspicious, she asked, "When you say it worked, what exactly do you mean?"

Leveraging lessons learned from my previous Groucho's disaster, I answered, "Liz, I don't think lunch at Groucho's is the most romantic place to get into all that. Why don't we wait for a better time? Is that OK?"

"Well, sure," she said seemingly pleased, but curious.

Kayla arrived with our drinks and sandwiches, placing them in front of us.

"See?" said Elizabeth, smiling and pointing to her turkey sandwich. "No bacon!"

The rest of our lunch went so well that over the next week, we slowly began returning to normal. But I made a conscious effort to create a new normal. I bought her flowers – twice – and had them delivered to her work so she would have witnesses to her boyfriend's thoughtfulness. I also sent her several sweet or silly text messages for no reason, something I realized I'd been negligent about. We talked every day, made dinner together, and took Bono for walks around my neighborhood. But I knew the Big Question, the one I had successfully dodged the second time at Groucho's, was still looming. And knowing Elizabeth carried lifelong dreams of the ideal engagement proposal set the bar pretty high. I needed ideas. Anything that didn't involve me singing.

TWENTY-SIX

Convergence

Following my do-over lunch with Elizabeth, my father and I arranged to meet at his coffee shop early the next morning to catch up on his story. We had met eight times during the two weeks I was now living over again, but I didn't see the need to repeat those sessions one for one. As my father said on the way to the doctor, a few summary review efforts should suffice. But he did need to finish his story for me.

Arriving at the café shortly after eight, I spotted my dad standing with another gentleman about his age next to the condiment counter. Not wanting to interrupt their conversation, I wandered toward the community table to get set up, but my father saw me and waved me toward him. I left my laptop on the table and made my way over.

"Son, I want you to meet someone," he said. "This is Dr. Braden LeClair."

I extended my hand as his name bounced around inside my head. "From the Sole Winners?" I asked as I shook his hand.

"Wow," he said, laughing, "it's been a long time since someone recognized me for that. It's nice to meet you, Daniel."

"Braden is a professor in the university's school of music," my father explained. "He's also one of my daily guests in the café."

"Daily *addicts* is more like it," said Braden with a grin. "Phillip, I've got to run. It was good to see you both."

"Nice to meet you," I said, still a little stunned as he walked away. I turned to my dad and said, "That was really weird."

197

"Why is that?"

"I don't know," I said as we moved across the café toward the table. "It's like meeting the tooth fairy or something."

"Son, everyone in my story was a real person. You have to know that by now."

"I do, but still. It's just weird. Do you keep in touch with anyone else we've talked about?"

"Well, Zack Flynn, the guitarist from the Sole Winners, is also on the faculty at the university. He teaches guitar."

"You guys should get back together for a reunion tour," I joked as I took my seat at the table. "Everyone else is doing it these days."

My dad laughed as he sat down next to me. "We'd have to call it 'The *Old* Winners Tour.'"

"It's a shame Greene Streets isn't still around," I said. "It would have been fun to see you guys play a gig there."

As I opened my laptop and got settled, I noticed a blank look on my dad's face as his eyes stared out the window. "You OK, Dad?" I asked, snapping him out of his trance.

"Huh?" he asked, a little startled.

Given his memory issues, I couldn't help but ask, "Did you take your medicine this morning?"

He huffed and said, "Oh, no. Not you, too."

"What do you mean?"

"That's the first thing your mother asked me this morning when she came in the kitchen," he said, shaking his head. "Please don't do that to me."

"I'm sorry, Dad. I just saw you thinking and…"

"I had an idea come to me, that's all."

"Ah, anything good?"

He smiled and said, "You'll have to wait."

I knew that was my cue to move on. "You ready to get back to our story, then?"

"Not so fast," he said. "Before we get into all that, I want to hear about your visit to Santa Rosa. We're both Black Hole alumni, now."

I laughed and said, "We should get t-shirts or something."

"I'll have some made up," he joked. "So, how did it go?"

"Honestly, it was the scariest thing I've ever done. I don't know how you did that twice."

"Well, the first time I was young and stupid. The second time I was stupid and drunk, so…"

"You weren't scared of animals hiding in there, like wolves or mountain lions or something?"

"No, I guess I didn't really think about that."

"Man, I did."

"But you did it anyway. And that took courage. I'm proud of you, Son. And thankful."

"Thanks, Dad. I'm glad I had the chance to help you."

We spent the next hour recreating my notes on my laptop as we talked through everything from his first audition through his second trip to Black Hole. I knew I would need to spend a fair amount of time over the next two weeks turning my notes back into our written story. But I also needed to know how it ended. "So, what happened after you left Santa Rosa?" I asked.

"Hang on one sec," said my dad as he took a call on his phone. "It's your mother."

While my father talked with my mom about something he apparently forgot to do, I scrolled through my notes looking for holes in the story.

My dad said goodbye to my mother, then turned to me and asked, "Can you follow me over to our house? I've got to do something for your mother real quick."

"Sure. Anything wrong?"

"Her bathroom sink is clogged. I told her yesterday I'd fix it this morning before she got in there, but I forgot. It won't take five minutes, then we can get back to your questions."

I had nothing else planned for the day, so I agreed. However, his clogged sink repair, which involved using his gas-powered pressure washer to force water down the drain, took a little longer than five minutes. While he took care of the sink, I kept my mother company in the kitchen.

"Thank you again for taking him to the doctor yesterday," she said.

"Well, you can thank Elizabeth. She set that up for us."

"I'm so glad you two are together again."

Since I hadn't told my mother anything about my lunch with Elizabeth, it was obvious they'd been talking. "She told you that, I assume."

"We traded texts after your lunch yesterday."

"I see," I said, waiting for her to steer our conversation toward a possible proposal.

"So, what's next for you two?" she asked.

"Oh, you know, the usual."

"Daniel, honestly. You're going to lose that girl if you don't do something about it."

"You know Mom, you're probably right about that."

"Then you're going to propose?"

I laughed, "If I was, you're the last person I'd tell."

My dad ran through the kitchen and into the garage. A moment later the sound of the gas motor outside stopped. "Does he have to do this often?" I asked.

"A couple times a year," she said. "Getting him to call a plumber is like getting him to see a doctor."

After my dad finished with the sink, my mother disappeared into her bathroom for her morning get-ready-for-the-day ritual while he joined me at the kitchen table.

"OK, where were we?" he said, wiping his hands on a paper towel.

"You woke up in your five-dollar motel room in Santa Rosa for the third time and headed home."

"That's right," he said. "I picked up my car from the garage across the street, filled my tank full of gas, and headed east. I didn't care about anything but just getting home."

ಬಿಲ

The only stops Phillip made on his drive home to Columbia were for gas and Pepsi. His bag of Nekot cookies lasted until Nashville but he refused to stop for food or sleep. Monday afternoon, thirty-one hours after leaving the truck stop in Santa Rosa, he opened the front door of his apartment, stepped into his empty den, and fell to his knees on the hardwood floor. Hanging his head from his shoulders, he closed his eyes, rolled onto his back, and fell sound asleep.

When the growling of Phillip's empty stomach woke him three hours later, his eyes opened to a view of peeling paint on his plaster ceiling. After a moment of disorientation, a smile crept across his face. He was home.

ಬಿಲ

"So, Gina obviously broke up with you again after you didn't go through with the audition."

"Yep."

"Did you call her when you got back?"

"No. When I woke up from my nap on the floor, the red light was blinking on my answering machine. She left an angry message to let me know we were through and that I was out of the band after our gig that Friday."

"That was kind of cold."

"Yeah, well. It was Gina. At least I wasn't surprised. Or upset about it."

"Did you play the gig on Friday? Because you knew Vallie would be there."

"I did. And just like the first time, it changed everything."

❧

When Phillip arrived at Michael's rented duplex late Friday afternoon to help load their equipment into Zack's van, his bandmates were already there, standing outside the garage. They greeted him with silent, knowing stares as he made his way toward them.

"Hey, guys," said Phillip.

"Hey, Phillip," said Braden, speaking for the group.

"I'm guessing you guys heard the news," said Phillip, stopping a few feet away.

"You chickened out and got dumped," said Michael.

Unbothered by Michael's mocking attitude, Phillip simply said, "I did, Michael. And this is my last show with you guys tonight."

"Oh, darn," Michael said sarcastically.

Phillip studied the smug grin on his drummer's face. "You know, Michael, there's something I've been wanting to say to you."

"Yeah? What's that?"

Phillip smiled and said, "You're a really great drummer. And I'm lucky I got to play with you guys."

Braden took a step toward Phillip and shook his hand. "Sorry about everything, man," he said.

"Thanks, Braden. But I'm hoping we can put on a really good show tonight."

"I'm in," said Zack, offering his hand to Phillip.

After shaking Zack's hand, Phillip turned and offered his hand to Michael.

Michael paused for a moment, then stepped forward and gripped Phillip's hand. "Good luck tonight, man," he said.

"Thanks, Michael," said Phillip. Taking a step back, Phillip said to the group, "Guys, there's a song I'd like to do tonight that you haven't heard before. Could I play it real quick for you?"

After a few confirming nods, Phillip ran to his car and retrieved his guitar. There on the driveway, he played what he planned to sing as Vallie's request song.

"Where did you hear that?" asked Braden.

"I wrote it," said Phillip.

"You wrote that?" asked a surprised Michael.

"I know Gina doesn't like us doing country songs, but do you think you guys could back me up on this one tonight?"

Phillip watched the three exchange looks before Zack said, "We've got you covered, bro."

The crowd at Greene Streets was as big as Phillip had ever seen at the venue. But having played the Astrodome, he felt no pressure as he took the stage. While he and the band worked their way through the first set, Phillip kept his eyes out for Vallie. And after performing U2's song *New Year's Day*, Phillip looked down to see Vallie's roommate waving him over to the edge of the stage. Kneeling down to her, just as he did before, he asked, "Do you have a request for me?"

"I want you to sing a song to my friend," she said. "I'm trying to keep her from driving to Charleston to see her boyfriend tonight."

"What's your friend's name?" he asked as if he didn't know.

"It's Vallie."

"I've got a nice country song for her," said Phillip.

"Oh, good. She likes that. And make sure you look at her when you sing. Sing it to her." Holding up a ten-dollar bill, she added, "And I'll give you ten bucks if you come talk to her."

"Keep your money," said Phillip, looking up to find Vallie.

"We're over there," she said pointing up and to her left.

"Got it," said Phillip, rising to his feet. He turned to his band and said, "Guys, the song I played on the driveway. The one I wrote." After receiving wave from Michael and nods from Zack and Braden, Phillip stepped toward the microphone. He found Vallie's face in the crowd and said, "This next song is for you, Vallie. I hope you follow your heart."

Phillip turned around to face his band and began strumming the first chords of *Escape*. The rest of the band joined in with ease as if they had heard it a hundred times. Stepping up to the microphone, Phillip watched Vallie's beautiful face as he sang the words he wrote for her.

> *Time stole you away from me*
> *But someday I know*
> *My song will bring you back to me*
> *I'll go where you go*
> *I'd leave this dark and lonely cave*
> *If only I could be so brave*
>
> *Please guide my way*
> *I just can't stay*
> *Let's leave today*
> *Come with me*

With the song over and the audience roaring its approval, Phillip turned to Braden. Leaning to his ear he said, "That's it for me, man. I'm done."

Without replying, Braden shook Phillip's hand, pulling him close for a brief hug. Phillip pointed to Michael behind the drums and gave him a thumbs-up before shaking hands with Zack. "Bye guys; it's been fun," he said, leaving the stage with his guitar on his back.

Once on the floor, Phillip looked up into the crowd to find Vallie staring down at him behind the second-tier railing, her face beaming with excitement. He offered a gentle wave of his hand, then turned and walked through the side door exit and out into the night.

ல్యు

"Wait, you left?" I asked, incredulous. "You didn't go talk to her? After all that? She was right there!" I admit I may have gotten a little too caught up in the story.

"Son, if you had seen the look of hurt and fear on her face there in Albuquerque when she thought she might lose Del, you'd understand. She belonged with him. And I wasn't going to mess that up again. Because I cared about her, I had to let her go."

"So, that's it? That's the end of the story?"

"Well, not quite."

ல్యు

As Phillip started down the empty sidewalk under the street lights, he heard a female voice calling after him.

"Wait!" she said.

He turned around to see Vallie's roommate.

She stopped and asked, "Where are you going?"

Phillip shrugged. "To get a cup of coffee, I guess," he said. He began to turn away, but then added, "You want to come with me?"

The girl hesitated, looked back toward Greene Streets, then smiled and stepped toward him.

"What's your name?" Phillip asked as they began to walk together.

"Donna. What's yours?"

"Phillip. Phillip Johnson."

∽✦∾

"That's a coincidence," I said, referring to the girl's name.

"Not really," said my dad. "Wait here one sec."

I waited at the kitchen table until my dad returned carrying yet another piece of paper from his study. He placed it on the table in front of me.

"That's Donna," he said.

"That's Mom!" I shouted. "What the…"

My dad said nothing, letting my brain catch up with his story.

"So…Mom was Vallie's roommate the whole time?" I finally surmised.

He nodded. "Vallie was your mom's maid of honor at our wedding. She and her husband, Del, flew in from Dallas to be there."

"They lived in Dallas? Is that how they were at your concert in Albuquerque?"

"Yep. After Vallie and Del got married, he landed a job with Frito Lay at their headquarters out there. It's just a short flight to Albuquerque. So, when I heard they moved to Texas, it finally made sense."

With my mind still trying to grasp everything, I asked, "So, after you walked out of Greene Streets, was that the coffee date with Mom I've always heard about?"

"That was it. We've been together ever since."

"And this picture you drew of her, what was that from?"

"I drew that from a photo taken at Vallie's wedding. It's always been one of my favorites."

I sat there in thought for a moment, trying to make sense of it all. Over the last three months, the story that seemed so ridiculous that I worried about my dad's sanity had slowly revealed itself to be true. Time travel included. And in the end, all the pieces fit with what I had known all my life.

"So," I said, "I guess we can say this is really a story about how you met Mom."

He smiled. "In a nutshell, sure."

"That's a pretty crazy nutshell," I said.

He looked down at his drawing of my mother and said, "It was worth every bit of it."

TWENTY-SEVEN

Opportunity

Over the next few days, I continued working to recapture my dad's story. When necessary, I'd give him a call or send him a text with a question, just to make sure I remembered things correctly. I had a fair amount of writing still ahead of me, but I was determined to get it off my plate before school started in less than two weeks. On Wednesday morning, he sent me a text message asking to meet me for lunch at Market on Main. It was an unusual request. My dad and I don't normally do lunch. So, I assumed he was up to something.

We met on Main Street in front of the restaurant at eleven-thirty. When the hostess greeted us at the front door, my father requested that we sit outside in their courtyard. Coincidentally, we sat at the same table where Elizabeth and I had lunch. Or will have lunch the next week. If I ask her again. While I tried to sort out the time travel order of things in my head, I heard my dad say, "I have an opportunity for you."

When I was growing up, that usually meant work of some kind. "What kind of opportunity?" I asked, as I began looking over the menu.

"Remember when you and I joked about a Sole Winners reunion?" he asked.

"Sure. Why, are you thinking about doing that?"

"It's in the works," he said. "I've been talking with Braden and Zack, and they're in."

"Nice!"

"And they have a drummer friend who can sub for Michael."

"Where is Michael?" I asked.

"No one knows. He moved back to Maryland after school, and we lost touch with him."

"So, are you guys going to do a show somewhere?"

"That's the plan. We've already practiced a couple of times."

Our server interrupted, politely, to take our orders. While I ordered a crab cake BLT, my dad got some kind of fancy lobster sandwich. I was thankful he had offered to pay for lunch. After she left us, I picked up our conversation. "You've been pretty stealthy, Dad. I had no idea you were getting the band back together."

"I needed to get a feel for it before I said anything. But I'm pretty excited."

"So, when is all this happening?"

"Well, the other guys are professional musicians, so it's really up to me to dust off the cobwebs and get ready."

"You said you had an opportunity for me. How does that tie into your reunion tour?"

He laughed and said, "Let's not call it a tour. But I know the owner here, and he's going to let us play next Thursday night, right here in the outdoor courtyard."

"Here? That's so cool! You know, the last time I was here they had some college kid up there with an acoustic guitar singing solo. It reminded me of you."

"Well, that's kind of in line with what I wanted to talk with you about."

"What, do you need my help setting up or something?"

"No, Son," he said smiling. "I want you to think *bigger.*"

"Um, you want me to do the lights for your show?"

"Daniel, this is your chance to sing to Elizabeth."

There are certain rare stress-induced occasions when words come out of my mouth unfiltered that aren't part of my usual vocabulary. I'm embarrassed to say this was one of those times. But the gist of my response was an emphatic "no."

Undeterred, my dad continued, "Daniel, listen to me. You want to propose, don't you?"

My desire to propose wasn't the issue. "Sure, but–"

"And you want it to be more romantic than your Groucho's fail, don't you?"

He had me there; I gave a silent nod.

"So, here's what I'm thinking: That song you told me about, the one you sang when you met Elizabeth, we can include that in our set."

"No, Dad."

"You can bring her to our show – she would never suspect anything – and then when we start playing the song you can come up and sing it to her."

"Dad, no."

"Then when you're done, you just pop the question in front of everyone. She'll love it, I promise! What do you think?"

Conceptually, it wasn't a bad idea. And he was right; Elizabeth would love it. But as I imagined the scene my dad described, my heart felt like it was going to explode in my chest.

"Are you OK, Son? You're looking a little pale."

"I'm fine," I said, taking a deep breath. "I just need a sec."

"Oh, and one more thing," he said. "And this was your mother's idea–"

"Mom?" That spiked my blood pressure all over again. "You think Mom can keep this a secret, Dad? I bet she's brainstorming ideas with Elizabeth right now!"

"Easy, Son." He looked around to see if we were drawing attention from other tables. Then in a calming voice, he said, "I know your mom talks with Elizabeth, but she knows how special this can be for the two of you. She doesn't want to ruin it or interfere in any way, I promise."

Lowering my voice to normal conversation level, I said, "Well, sorry, but I'll need a little more assurance than that."

My dad smiled. Trying to lighten the mood, he asked, "Would a signed confidentiality agreement do?"

"Is it notarized?" I asked, straight-faced.

"Daniel, I think you're overreacting just a bit. But if it makes you feel better, ask your mom yourself. And I'll let her tell you about her idea."

"Fine," I said, trying to hide the stress I knew was showing on my face. I looked away, but I could tell my dad was studying me.

"Are you OK?" he asked.

"I'm fine," I said with a little less zing.

"You know, I was really hoping you'd be excited about this idea."

"Dad, I appreciate what you're trying to do. I do. Really. But what you're asking would be a huge leap for me. And I don't think I can pull it off."

My dad sat quietly for a moment while I looked toward the small, open, concrete stage floor. I tried to picture myself singing to a courtyard full of people. And Elizabeth. All I could see was a disaster waiting to happen.

"I tell you what," my dad finally said. "Come to rehearsal with me. You can practice the song with the band with no one watching and see how you feel. If you don't think you'd be comfortable singing at our show, then don't do it. Simple as that. What do you think?"

It seemed like a fair compromise. At least I wasn't committing to anything. "I guess I can do that," I said sheepishly as our server arrived with our sandwiches. The food looked good, but I didn't feel as hungry as I did a few minutes before.

My dad took a sip from his glass of water, put his hand on my arm, and said, "Son, listen. Whenever you doubt yourself, I want you to remember something. You're the guy who walked into a dark cave full of wolves to save his dad."

"But there weren't any wolves in there," I countered.

"You didn't know that when you stepped in, did you?"

With that, a new smile of confidence spread across my face. I took a big bite of my crab cake BLT and said, "When's our first rehearsal?"

TWENTY-EIGHT

Ring of Truth

Before I could get home from lunch with my dad, I received a call from my mother. He had obviously tipped her off to my confidentiality concern, and she jumped straight to the point. She promised that she had not – and would not – reveal any proposal plans to Elizabeth. She then ended the call abruptly, saying she had clothes in the dryer. While I appreciated the call, my knowledge of her previous conspiracy with Elizabeth (i.e., "the break"), combined with her quick non-emergency exit off the phone, led me to steer my car toward their house instead of mine. My mother's never been able to look at me when she's hiding something. It's an obvious tell I've enjoyed exploiting around Christmas and birthdays, but the stakes were now higher than a new video game or bicycle. I needed her assurance in person.

She had seen my car pull into their driveway and was waiting expectantly in the kitchen when I entered from the garage. My anxiety had grown on the way over, and I mentally prepared myself for an argument.

"Well, hello!" she said happily. "I wasn't expecting to see you this afternoon."

"Just thought I'd say hi," I said, dropping my keys and phone onto the counter. Aside from my deceptive greeting, I wasted no time diving into the confrontation. "Mom–"

"I was just about to have a cup of coffee," she said, interrupting. "Would you like to join me? It's a new medium roast from Tanzania your father just started offering. It's yummy. I think you'll actually like this one."

The thought of sipping a nice cup of coffee with my mother was surprisingly disarming. "That sounds great," I said, tabling my agenda for the moment.

We settled at the kitchen table with our cups of coffee. Like my father, I drank mine black. Good coffee doesn't need help, he always said. After a careful sip, I took a moment to process my sensory experience, swooshing the coffee around in my mouth. I discovered a buttery, slightly smokey flavor with just a hint of nuttiness. It had medium body and a smooth finish. I gave it an A minus. It was officially drinkable. Now more relaxed, I decided to approach my proposal concerns in a more subtle, conversational fashion.

"So, Mom, you didn't give me a chance on the phone to ask about Dad's big reunion show."

"Oh, I'm so excited!" she said. "I've already told so many people. My best friend from college and her husband are going to be there."

"Vallie?" I asked.

She looked surprised. "You know about Vallie?"

I gave a dismissive shrug as I lifted my cup. "I think Dad mentioned her once, yeah."

My mother gave me that knowing look of hers. "He did, huh?"

I sipped my coffee and pretended to be distracted by the flavor. "This is really good; where is it from again?"

"Africa," she said, unblinking. "What did your father say about Vallie?"

"Oh, just that she was your roommate or something in college and that she was in your wedding."

She looked down and thoughtfully ran her finger along the curving handle of her white porcelain coffee cup. "You know," she said after a moment, "I think your father's always had a little crush on Vallie. Did he tell you that, too?"

"No, of course not," I lied.

"He even drew a picture of her once when we were in school. I think it's still here in the house somewhere."

I ignored the bait and asked, "Did it bother you? That he liked her?"

"Oh, I used to kid him about it. He always denied it, of course. But I understood. Vallie was...let's just say boys were always falling for Vallie. But I knew your father loved me. Besides, Vallie only had one boy in mind, and that was the man she married, Del. Which is funny, because I tried to talk her out of it."

"How come?"

"I just didn't think he was right for her. In fact, the night I met your father, I was trying to keep her from going to see Del in Charleston. We were at your father's show in Five Points, and Vallie wanted to leave and drive down there. So, I went up to the stage and asked your father to sing a song for her to help keep her there with me. She loved country music, so I was hoping he knew some. I even offered him money if he'd come down and talk to her. But he wouldn't take it; I liked him for that. He turned down twenty dollars."

I slipped and said, "I thought it was ten."

Slightly taken aback, she asked, "He's told you this already?"

I lifted my cup in front of my mouth and mumbled, "He must have mentioned it when he told me how y'all met."

"Uh-huh," she said, studying me. "He's obviously told you more than you're letting on."

"Just that Vallie got married and moved to Dallas. That's all."

"They used to live in Dallas, but they now live in Manning, where she grew up. They took over her father's furniture business when he passed away a few years ago."

"Oh, so that's how they can be at the show next week," I gathered.

"That's right."

We sat for a moment sipping our coffee. It seemed like a harmless time to discuss the possibility of my upcoming proposal. "So, Mom, about the show, you're sure you haven't said anything to Elizabeth about me proposing? Because I'm still not sure about it, yet."

She looked at me squarely in the eyes and said, "Son, I told you, I haven't. I promise I wouldn't do that."

She passed the test with flying colors. "Thanks, Mom," I said with a sigh of relief. "Now I just have to figure out what to do about a ring," I added.

"I think I might be able to help you there," she said, getting up from the table. She walked down the hall to their bedroom and came back with a small cube-shaped box in the palm of her hand. "Here," she said, handing it to me.

"What's this?" I asked. I opened the box to find a perfectly shaped diamond mounted on a simple gold band.

"That was my grandmother's wedding ring. What do you think?"

"It's beautiful, Mom. But I could never afford something this nice."

"It'll probably need resizing," she said.

"Wait, what are you saying?"

She smiled warmly and said, "It's yours, Son."

Still trying to grasp what was happening, I asked, "Are you saying I can give this to Elizabeth? As an engagement ring?"

"Daniel, I've been saving that ring until you found the right girl. And Elizabeth is like a daughter to me. I would love to see my sweet grandmother's ring on her finger."

"Wow," is all I could say as I sat staring at the ring in the box. "I don't know how I could ever thank you enough, Mom."

"Marry her. That's thanks enough. Oh, and I have one more idea for you. It involves roses. Lots and lots of roses."

TWENTY-NINE

History Lesson

The week leading up to the Sole Winners reunion concert at Market on Main, I rehearsed with my dad and his band three times. Their new drummer, Michael's replacement, was a quiet but amazingly skilled percussionist named Colin, a graduate student. Since Braden and Zack were both university professors, we were able to use one of the school's soundproof practice rooms, which eased some of my anxiety about anyone hearing me. But I learned quickly that pretending you're on *American Idol* in your car is a lot different than singing solo into a microphone. The sound of my voice instead of Edwin McCain's left me wondering if I'd get booed off stage before I even had a chance to propose to Elizabeth.

"Dad, I still don't know if I can do this," I said during our first rehearsal. And before I could stop the words from coming out of my mouth, I added, "How in the world did you play the Astrodome?"

"The Astrodome?" asked Braden, looking at my dad.

My dad chuckled uncomfortably while cutting his eyes at me. "He obviously meant that in a metaphorical sense. You know, large crowds can make you nervous. That sort of thing."

"Right," I said. "I meant to say how *would* you sing on a stage like that. All those people looking at you. I think I'd just freeze."

"Daniel, here's a bit of advice," said Zack. "I tell my students this all the time. Find one friendly face in the crowd before you start. One smiling face looking at you. And simply smile back at them. Don't worry or think about anyone else. Sing or play to that one person like they're the only one there."

"Either that or keep your eyes closed and find your happy place," said Braden. "You'd be amazed how many performers do that."

"Son, do you remember what I told you about my first performance at Greene Streets? When it was just me up on stage."

"You closed your eyes and imagined you were playing at home by yourself," I said.

"That's right. And then when I opened them, I saw Gina looking up at me. So, I just sang the rest of my set to her. I didn't know who she was, but it eased my nerves to just sing to a pretty, smiling face."

"Wait," said Braden, "you didn't know Gina the first time you played at Greene Streets?"

"No, that's how I met her. She watched me perform, then we talked after."

"That's it?" asked Braden. "She told me her dad's record company was behind the whole thing."

"Her dad's record company?" my dad repeated. "She told you that?"

"That's right," said Zack. "That's why we all agreed to be in the band."

"But when you ditched the audition," added Braden, "they dumped us."

My dad held up his hands calmly and said, "Guys, first of all, this is ancient history. But it sounds like Gina was just being Gina. She wanted to manage a band, so she lied to get one."

"But what about the audition in L.A.?" asked Zack. "She said that was just a formality."

"Her dad called in a few favors with people he knew to get me an audition," my dad explained, "but it was just to make Gina happy. That was it. He had nothing to do with our band. Besides, you think some kid playing an acoustic cover of *Pink Houses* is going to land a record deal for a band in South Carolina? I probably wouldn't have made it past the first verse." My dad looked at me discreetly and winked.

Zack shook his head. "I wish we had known all that. Poor Michael."

"What do you mean?" asked my dad.

"Gina filled Michael's head with all kinds of ideas about him being a rock star," explained Braden.

"Then she dropped him like a rock when she graduated," added Zack.

"I can only imagine what she told him," said my dad solemnly.

As the three former Sole Winners sat with glazed looks on their faces pondering Gina's many manipulations, I tried to lighten the mood. "Well, on that happy note," I said, "can I try singing *I'll Be* one more time?"

THIRTY

Like a Dream

When I told Elizabeth about my dad's old band playing a one-night-only gig at Market on Main, she was shocked. To fully explain it, I had to give a quick time-travel-free summary of his life as a twenty-year-old college dropout musician wannabe. Not surprisingly, the image I painted of my dad in his youth didn't match the quiet, unassuming man she had come to know over the previous two years. The disconnect only served to create more intrigue over his upcoming performance. She made sure to be off work that Thursday and told all her friends to be there.

When the big day arrived, I offered to help the band set up their equipment and just have Elizabeth meet me at MOM, but my dad said no. He said I should give her the appearance of being on a normal date to further the surprise when I joined the band on stage. I trusted his instincts over mine.

The show was scheduled for seven o'clock. The courtyard at MOM has two rows of large picnic tables with bench seats directly before the stage. Regular tables and chairs are scattered around the rest of the astroturf ground cover. My father had arranged for the front and center picnic table to be reserved in my name, for which I was thankful given the large Thursday night crowd. When Elizabeth and I arrived around six-fifteen for dinner, my mother was already seated at our table.

"Hey, Mom," I said as we joined her. Thinking ahead to my proposal logistics, I made sure Elizabeth sat on the end of the picnic bench closest to the stage. "Where's Dad?" I asked.

"Oh, he was here a minute ago," my mother said glancing around. "He's off doing band stuff, I suppose. Are you kids hungry?"

"I am," Elizabeth said, picking up a menu. She elbowed me and asked, "What are you having?"

"The scallops," I said, glancing at the first thing on the menu.

"We can't both get the same thing," she said, her eyes still scanning the menu. "I'll get the scallops; you get something else. Then we'll share."

I'm normally not big on sharing my food, but I wanted her to be happy, that night in particular. Besides, with my mind racing ahead to my public singing debut, I really wasn't that hungry. "I tell you what," I said, "you just pick two things you like and order for both of us."

Judging from all the equipment on stage, it appeared the band was ready to play, but I didn't see my dad or the other Sole Winners anywhere. As I scanned the courtyard, I felt a drip of perspiration roll down my temple. While it may have been a nervous sweat, we were sitting outside on a typically hot, humid August night in Columbia. Were it not for two large fans blowing air across the dining area, it may have been unbearable. But the persistent breeze kept us relatively cool and the mosquitos away.

After a short wait, our server arrived with glasses of water, ready to take our order. Elizabeth chose the truffle pasta for me to share with her scallops.

"So, Donna," said Elizabeth to my mother, "Daniel told me about Phillip and his band from back in college and how you two met. I bet you're really excited to see him on stage again."

"I'm probably more surprised than anything," answered my mom. "I didn't know he was putting this together until last week. He's kind of sneaky that way sometimes." She smiled and added, "But I love him."

"Well, I'm excited," I said. Then, supporting my new theory that time travel makes you stupid, I added. "I hope he does some of his songs."

"What songs?" my mother asked, with a curious look.

I scrambled to think of a non-Walker Owens explanation for yet another unwitting alternate timeline reference. "Oh, you know…like the one he wrote for your birthday." Nice save, I thought as I allowed myself to exhale.

"Daniel told me about that," said Elizabeth. "That was so sweet."

"I just hope he doesn't play it here," my mother said. "I might cry." She suddenly became very excited as she looked toward the entrance to the courtyard.

I turned to see an older, rather plump couple about my parents' age heading our way. Following my mother's lead, Elizabeth and I stood as they approached our table. My mother hugged both of them before turning to us. She always enjoyed formal introductions.

"Daniel and Elizabeth," she said, extending her arm toward our guests, "I want you to meet my dear friend Vallie Boykin and her husband, Del. Vallie and Del, this is my son, Daniel, and his girlfriend, Elizabeth."

We exchanged "nice to meet you" greetings before taking our seats at the picnic table. As I studied Vallie's overly round,

227

smiling face, I struggled to reconcile what I was seeing with everything I had heard, not to mention my dad's drawing.

"So, how's life in Manning?" asked my mother.

"Oh, it's still the same," said Vallie. "Not much changes in Manning."

"I honestly never thought you'd end up there," said my mom.

"Well, that makes two of us," said Vallie. She glanced at Del, smiled, and added, "Make that three of us."

"Are your twin sisters still there?"

"No, Julie lives in Chicago, and Janice lives in Atlanta. Life can be funny sometimes."

As our server arrived with our dinner, my mom asked Vallie, "Did y'all want to order something?"

"No," said Vallie, "We had something on the way into town. I can never pass a Chick-fil-A without stopping for nuggets and a milkshake."

While Elizabeth and I shared our entrées quietly, my mom continued to catch up with her old friends. I was thankful for the distraction, which when combined with my truffle pasta and one of Elizabeth's two scallops, helped calm my nerves. Just as I scooped the last of Elizabeth's sauteed green beans off her plate, the Sole Winners took the stage. Everyone – at our table at least – gave a rousing welcome applause.

"Good evening," said my dad into the center stage microphone. "We are the Sole Winners. That's s-o-l-e if you were wondering. We're glad to be back after a forty-year break and hope you enjoy the show."

My father had shared that the band had quite a bit of debate regarding which songs to include in their setlist. While my dad wanted to revive their original 80s pop rock covers, Braden and Zack preferred more current hits. Colin had no opinion. Since my father hadn't heard any of the songs Zack sampled on guitar, nor did he have the time or interest to learn them, he held firm until Braden and Zack gave in. Their first song was, of course, *Pink Houses* by John Cougar Mellencamp.

I realized as I watched my dad perform that we had neglected to agree on when my song would come up in their set. So as each song ended, my heart would pound in my chest while I sat wondering if I was on next. But after an hour of that stress roller coaster, I finally became numb to it. And that's when I heard the opening chords of *I'll Be*. My dad smiled and waved me up.

Elizabeth turned to me and said, "That's our song!"

I gave her a quick kiss, let go of her hand, and rose to my feet.

"Where are you going?" she asked.

With the stage less than ten feet from our table, I didn't have time to answer. I hopped onto the concrete platform and positioned myself behind the mic. Remembering Zack's advice, I looked straight at Elizabeth and ignored everyone else. Her wide eyes and disbelieving smile were all I wanted to see. And when Zack finished the short guitar intro, I began to sing.

Elizabeth screamed with excitement, then gave into laughter, and finally settled into a mesmerizing stare that almost made me forget the words to the song.

After making it through the second verse and chorus without a mistake, I decided not to press my luck any further. Rather than sing the bridge, I stepped down from the stage while the band kept playing and approached Elizabeth. Pulling my great-grandmother's ring from my pocket, I knelt down on my right knee before her at the picnic table. Holding the ring up to her, I asked simply, "Will you marry me?"

"Yes!" she shouted, jumping up from the table and into my arms. As we held each other tightly and swayed to the music, a shower of rose petals fell all around us. That was my mother's idea. She arranged for two MOM staffers to toss the petals into the air before the large fans once they were sure Elizabeth had said yes. I cupped my hands on Elizabeth's cheeks and looked into her joyful, tear-filled eyes.

"It's just like a dream," she said.

I kissed her gently as our song came to an end. My mother was the first one to us. As I gave room to the crowd of women and girls wanting to hug Elizabeth and see her ring, I felt a hand on my shoulder.

"Congratulations, Son," my dad said, giving me a bear hug. "You sounded great up there."

"Thank you, Dad. I owe you so much for making all this happen."

"It took both of us," he said. With a wink he added, "And a little help from Black Hole."

"You're the best, Dad." I hugged him one more time before my mom pulled me away.

"Did you like the roses?" she asked.

"That made the whole thing, Mom. Thank you."

"See how surprised Elizabeth was? Did you notice?"

"I did; she really was."

"And you thought I couldn't keep it a secret."

"I love you, Mom," I said, giving her a hug.

In the midst of all the laughs, hugs, and handshakes following our big moment, I lost track of Elizabeth. I finally spotted her, but seeing the look on her face, I didn't want to interrupt her conversation. Rather, I took out my phone and captured a picture of her talking to my amazing, time traveling dad. She was as happy as I'd ever seen her.

Shortly before our wedding three months later, I asked my dad if he would draw the picture I took of her that night as a wedding present. It's now framed and hanging in our sunroom.

My father didn't have the major stroke he suffered the first time. The mini strokes seemed to have stopped as well. He still misplaces his keys or glasses every now and then, but my mother and I worry a lot less than we used to. And since he's been on medication, Pumpkin has lost ten pounds.

Once I finished writing *The Ballad of Walker Owens*, as my dad titled his story, he let my mom read it while stressing heavily that it was mostly fiction. He didn't want to fight the same battle of truth he did with me. Elizabeth and I happened to be with my mom one Saturday afternoon in early October when she finished reading it. The three of us were relaxing on their back porch drinking iced tea when she closed her iPad and took off her reading glasses. Her only comment was, "I told you he had a crush on Vallie. Can I get anyone more tea?"

ABOUT THE AUTHOR

A native of South Carolina, Greg is a former IT professional and coffee shop owner. His four novels have received a total of twelve independent publishing book awards and honors. Having crafted relatable, realistic, and sometimes humorous character-driven stories in the Christian fiction genre with *A Seed for the Harvest* (2014) and *The Gills Creek Five* (2017), Greg explores coming-of-age themes in a 1974 summer beach setting in *The Sea Turtle* (2023). His latest award-winning work, *The Ballad of Walker Owens* (2024), is available in paperback, hardcover, Kindle, and Apple Books editions. While each of Greg's novels are unique in style and story, the savvy reader will note they share the same story universe.

Greg earned both his bachelor's and master's degrees from the University of South Carolina and lives in Columbia, SC with his wife and two dogs. Readers may visit Greg's website, gregmdodd.com, to stay current with news regarding his works. Thanks for reading.